CALLUM

BACKSTAGE SERIES

DANI RENÉ

You were no more damaged than you think you are,
In my eyes, that's where you were perfect.
Not for your outer appearance,
But for the beauty in your soul.
For the love in your heart.
And the light in your smile.
And I promise to spend my life showing you.

This book is for the dreamers.
You know who you are.
Those of you who want to do something
awesome with your life. Who don't give up.
Who fight for what you believe in.
We're all strong enough to do it.
The road may be long, filled with speed bumps,
but you always get to your destination.
Never give up. Work hard. Kick Ass.
And NEVER let anyone tell you you're not good
enough!
Because you fucking are!!
(Yeah I cursed, get over it!)

PROLOGUE

When you're the man every woman wants, the one they would drop their panties for in a heartbeat, no questions asked, *What do you do?*

I do what every other red-blooded man does. I take advantage. But what happens when you find one woman who changes the way you feel about yourself? Your life? And your heart?

Do you recognize the moment your life changes?

When you find clarity?

When the constant confusion you have becomes an untangled ball of string? The notes that are caught in your head for days on end suddenly play in an exquisitely constructed symphony.

That's what happened the day I laid eyes on her. When she slammed into me, spilling her milky cappuccino over my favorite white T-shirt. When chestnut eyes and sleek ice-blonde hair invaded my senses. Her sweet vanilla perfume engulfed my veins, and all I could see was the delicate angel.

My name is Callum Hayes.

I am a rock star, a rock god.

The tabloids call me a bad boy. They write the articles I want them to write. The image I portray is one of sex and rock 'n roll. Aren't rock stars meant to do that?

I'm sitting in my music room. The only place I can be myself. The real me nobody else sees. Images rush through my mind of what I crave to do to that gorgeous woman, distracting me from what I'm supposed to be doing.

Writing.

The want I feel for her is primal. I ache to bend her over this fucking piano, pull her tight little panties down her toned legs, and sink myself so deep inside that sexy little body, ruining her for any other man. I need her sweet pussy to mold only to my cock.

I want to make her yearn and ache for my mouth on her. My fingers inside her and my cock claiming her. Today was Tayla's second official day with us. She's got an ear for music and sound, which led her here, to our recording studio I set up in our home.

She's my brother's sound engineer, helping him set up the drum kit, aiding the other techs with tuning the guitars, and today, I've asked her to do mine. Nobody touches my baby, but I've allowed this beauty to lay her fingers on the instrument. She'll soon be on tour with us, and I can't wait to get her backstage.

My mind has been filled with dirty images since her interview. I turn my attention to the notebook; the words are jumbled, like the muddle in my mind. She will be the death of me. If I can't have her, I don't know what I'll do. Liam, my brother, is right. I put myself in situations like this, but this time feels different.

The way her sassy mouth challenges me makes me wish to see how much I can challenge her.

There is one thing he's mistaken about though. Tayla Quinn will be mine.

Beneath me.

Writhing. Moaning. Whimpering. Begging.

When I take her and make her scream my name, she'll ache only for me.

Callum fucking Hayes.

TAYLA

Los Angeles, the City of Angels, is my home. I grew up here. It's the only place that holds a part of me. The smog, the traffic, and the passionate, crazy people. And the hottest rock band in the world. Working for them would be a dream come true.

Since I've finished my sound engineering degree at UCLA, I'm ready to gain the experience I need to build my career. The thrill of getting my first gig is exciting.

When my parents migrated to London, I remained behind to complete my studies. My sister ventured off with them, studying fashion design at Cambridge. She's only three years younger than me, and I think that's allowed us to be friends rather than have sibling rivalry.

I grab the newspaper and a Coke, striding up to the cashier, placing my items on the counter. I watch her punch in the prices on the ancient register.

As I hand over the payment, I offer her a smile. With my drink and paper in hand, I make my way out of the store and down the street. I need to check airline prices since my folks have been pestering me about visiting. I traveled through Scotland and London over the past four years since they moved. To make friends out there was easy. I think it was the American accent. Everybody thought I was different; they asked questions about where I was from. They were always intrigued by the stories I could tell them.

Outside my apartment, I find my keys in my purse and unlock the door leading into a narrow entrance foyer. A quick look in my mailbox offers nothing but random flyers. My plan for the afternoon is to spend time online searching for a job. Anything would do at this point. Something that's not an option is waitressing. I am clumsy and would end up tripping with several plates in my hands.

My tiny apartment is pleasant and warm. I left the windows open this morning, and the sun rays shined through onto my second-hand sofa. One of those comfy ones, you know, that you can flop onto. Since I am not big into furniture, the apartment isn't cluttered. Besides the oak coffee table my parents bought, I have little else.

The bedroom is my sanctuary. It's the king-sized futon bed that keeps me sated. Especially on summer mornings when the sun floods through the window shining onto the bed, making it nearly impossible to get up. There's a boxed window seat which allows me to relax. Where I can write and compose songs. I am not an artist by any means, but I love playing my guitar. Or learning to. It' my most prized possession.

My laptop in hand, I power it on and get comfortable on the sofa. With my Coke on the table, I check out the newspaper first. There aren't normally many jobs in here, but I buy it anyway. It's a local paper, so at least there should be something close to home. Scanning the pages, I pull out my phone. An advertisement for an intern catches my attention. *Sound engineer, newly graduated.* I fit the prerequisites. There's no mention of who the band is, but this could be the opportunity I've been waiting for. As quickly as my screen is unlocked, I dial the number in the ad.

It rings twice, and I am about to hang up when someone answers. "You've reached Kierra Thorne. How may I help you?" *Kierra? Why does that name sound so familiar?*

"Yes, hello, uhm. My name is Tayla Quinn. I am calling about the internship you have advertised in the daily paper." My mind is whirling, and my hands are trembling. It's only a phone call, and I'm nervous. I can't imagine sitting in an interview.

"Yes, Tayla. The offer is an internship with the band. If you're free tomorrow, we can meet for coffee. If I am happy with you, I will bring you to meet the guys. The meeting will be a brief run through. There is a lot of information, so if we offer you the position, you will be required to dive in at the deep end."

"I'm free tomorrow." My voice is high pitched, and the excitement in my tone is unmistakable. "What time? I have most of the day open." She's silent for a moment, and I hear rustling.

"Tomorrow, ten a.m. Meet me at The Java Bean. Give me a shout when you arrive, and I'll find you."

"Perfect. Thank you, Kierra." As soon as I hang up, I drop my phone on the sofa and jump around in my living room. *What am I going to wear? Shit!* I need to call Emma. She'll know what to do.

With my laptop open, I log into my Skype account and message my sister. When she logs in, she'll get my message. I hope to God it's before tonight. As I lean backward, my eyes close. I recognize the name, Kierra. Oh God! I realize where I've heard it before. She's the assistant to Callum Hayes. *Holy shit.* This is huge. I could very well be an intern for Hunters in Oblivion.

It's nine forty-five. As I walk down the road, my heart is racing, and my palms are sweaty.

I pulled my long, blonde hair into a ponytail. Emma suggested I wear my skinny black jeans and a pastel blue, chiffon top. The sheer material is light, and the deeper blue tank top below covers what needs to be covered.

When I arrive at the small coffee shop, I take a deep breath and open the door. Pulling out my phone, I walk inside and hit dial on the number I now have saved in my contacts.

"Hello."

"Kierra, hi, it's Tay. I arrived."

"Great, I am behind you." Her giggle has me turning around to face the woman I recognize as the other half of Callum Hayes. She's been his assistant for roughly ten years, and seeing her in real life is unusual. I've lived in Los Angeles all my life, but I've never seen them out and about.

"It's so great to meet you." We shake hands as we step into the queue.

"I am so glad you called. I have testosterone overload in the goddamn house, and hopefully, I can persuade them to employ another woman." She gives me a pleasant, sincere smile, and my heart flutters at the prospect of being in the same room as either Hayes brother.

Once we've ordered our coffees, we find a small table in the rear of the shop. "So, tell me about you, Tayla. I need to understand the individual wanting the internship. Callum, I presume you know who he is?" I nod. "Well, he wants me to choose, and later, he will do the final interview."

"Okay, well I graduated top of my class. I've wanted to be in the entertainment industry since I can remember, but I prefer not to be in the spotlight. I like being in the background. Backstage." She nods.

"I understand. I hate it too, but with my position, I can't stop it happening." Her words take me back to the night I would rather forget. The night my life changed forever. Being in the spotlight will make it easier for him to find me if he ever tries. That can't happen. "And how do you feel about traveling? This job will include you working on tour with us." Dragging me back to the present, I glance at her.

"I love traveling. My parents live in London. I fly out to see them regularly. I have been fortunate to travel to other countries. Jetting off for a tour sounds perfect."

"It is, in some ways. In others, it's challenging. Remember, this work can be strenuous. No vacation. And Callum, he can be a pain in the ass. Don't tell him I said that." She snickers. Her long, mousy hair is loose and wavy. Her big blue eyes seem to peer right through me, and her petite frame makes her look fragile.

"I understand. Hard work and long nights are something I am used to, and I'm not scared of putting in one hundred percent." With a firm nod, she smiles, gets up, and glances around.

"Well, let's go."

"Now?"

"No time like the present, doll." With a wink, she turns and heads for the counter. Ordering another eight coffees, she grabs one Styrofoam tray and hands me the other. We head out onto the sidewalk when a black SUV pulls up, and a driver gets out and opens the door for us.

9

The interior is black leather, the windows are darkened, and we sit quietly as the car makes its way to a beautiful home in the Hollywood Hills that I recognize as home to the Hayes brothers. When we pull into the driveway, the nerves that were dormant for the trip immediately awaken. I'm unsure I can do this. I mean, this is massive.

Kierra rounds the car, and we made our way inside. The chatter in the house is electric. People are milling around, some on calls, others at makeshift desks. Being in the same vicinity as the crew has my head spinning. The surrounding air swirls with creativity. "Come on. He's presumably in the music room." We wade through the crowd, Kierra handing out the coffees as we go. She offers me one and keeps one for herself.

We wander up the stairs and into a room the same size as my apartment. It houses a piano, two guitars, three chairs, and a whiteboard up on the wall. I notice two remarkable sculptures in the corner of the room. One formed with wire, but I can't tell what it was. The other a clay bust.

"He's somewhere. Stay here. Let me try to find him." With that, I'm alone. Sipping my coffee, I take in my surroundings. The atmosphere in the room is surreal. It's filled with promise, creativity, and something I can't quite put my finger on.

A sound behind me startles me, and I whirl around, knocking into something solid my coffee spills everywhere, soaking the person

I've bumped into. The floor now has a large cup of coffee splashed on it, and the solid body I bumped into, wearing a tight, white T-shirt, is now stained brown.

"Shit! I am so sorry!" I peer up through my eyelashes and come face to face with his sky-blue eyes. Dumbstruck for a second and completely mesmerized. Of all the people in the universe, I could spill coffee on; it's *him*.

Heat flushes my cheeks and my pulse riots. I can't believe I'm standing just inches from him. The recognition is immediate. Short brown hair, those undeniably beautiful cerulean eyes, and a grin that can have any girl dropping her panties in seconds. The way his eyes crinkle at the edges sends a jolt of electricity over my skin, and anxiety churns deep in my stomach. He has the sexiest nose that crinkles when he smiles. I can't help but be starstruck. This was *the* Callum fucking Hayes.

"Don't worry about it, babe." His voice is raspy, and I realize he is still recovering from the flu. An amused expression crosses his handsome features. As he stares at me, I have the distinct feeling he wants to say more. Kierra walks in at that moment.

"Cal, I was looking for you. This is Tayla."

"Ki, two coffees for myself and Tayla, who seems to have had trouble keeping the coffee in her cup." Embarrassment courses through me, and I wish the ground would swallow me up. My face is crimson from the encounter. I glance up at him and struggle to slow my skittering pulse. Offering a small smile, I shake my head.

"You really don't have to. Let me clean this." As I point to the floor, he reaches out and touches my hand casually. My skin tingles at the contact. His touch is delicate yet commanding.

"It's on me. Literally." A wink has butterflies in my stomach waking and fluttering around. This is ridiculous. I want to work for him, and I can't even think straight when he's in front of me. "Thank you, Ki, I'll take it from here." She gives me a slight grin and mouths *good luck*.

"I'll bring the coffees up shortly." With that, the door clicks shut, and we're alone. It's only an interview. *Just breathe*. He grabs a chair and gestures for me to follow him.

"Sit." I do. He slides into the chair opposite me. "Tayla. Nice to meet you. I am Callum Hayes. I'm confident you know that." I nod. Words fail me. I'm embarrassing myself, and I don't know how to stop.

The door opens, and Kierra stands in the doorway with two cups of coffee. He rises and strolls toward her. I catch sight of his snug jeans hugging muscular thighs, and my mouth waters as my gaze notes how tight and sexy his ass is. God, this man is unbelievable.

I can understand why girls are constantly grabbing him. With his impeccable physique, there's no question about how attractive he is. I glance at myself and quickly feel inadequate to be in his company. I saw the girls he dated, they were supermodels, and I'm far from one of those. Merely five-four myself and a size ten, my long blonde hair falls midway down my back, and I have a soft, innocent face with dark brown eyes. Nothing remarkable here.

The click of the door draws me from my wayward thoughts. He wouldn't be interested in me anyhow. I'm here to work. Hopefully. When we're alone again, he joins me and passes me a mug with the band logo wrapped around the side. "Do you have any qualifications or experience?"

"Yes. I graduated top of my class. No experience. That's why I applied for an internship. Or even an entry-level job."

"Perfect. Experience is not a requirement. I prefer teaching my team the way I like things. Makes for an excellent working relationship when people do as I say. I am a perfectionist. Are you averse to traveling?" His eyes pierce into me, looking into my soul. I hope he doesn't see what is deep inside. The anxiety that still plagues me.

"No, my parents live in London, and I spend most holidays there. I have been to a few other countries, and I adore traveling. Being in a different country. Seeing the diversity of various cultures."

"Good answer. It's one of my favorite things too. To experience all that life can offer. So, what makes you assume you're worthy of working for Hunters?" His head cocks to the side, and frustration burns inside me. *Worthy? Are you serious?* I'm worthy of any position I want.

My blood boils that he could ask something like that. "I'm a hard worker. My head is screwed on straight. I don't do drugs, and I look after myself. I love music, I always have. The only thing I wanted since I can remember was to work in this convoluted fucking industry." I have no idea where the words come from, but they tumble from my lips. "The one where if you're a woman it's more difficult. It's a sexist industry, but I still want it. With a passion and fire that burns deep in my soul."

I don't know where that came from. My body is shaking. When he sits back, his gaze is so intense it unsettles me. There is a delight in his eyes as he enjoys making me angry.

"This was a bad idea. I'm sorry to have wasted your time," I babble on, and he watches me closely, not saying anything. The heat of his stare drinking me in sends my pulse into overdrive. The silence is heavy with a distinct tension.

He looks amused. My gaze drops to his hands. They look soft, smooth. His fingers have an elegance to them. Images of him strumming his guitar flit through my mind, and that doesn't relieve the knot of yearning in my stomach. "Thank you for the coffee, but—"

"You're quite a little wreck, aren't you, Tayla?" he remarks with a slow glance from my face to my hands and watches how I'm trembling. *Get a grip, Tayla, he's just a guy!*

"I need a job, and if someone doesn't find me worthy, they can shove it." The tirade is out of my mouth before I can think. My eyes snap up to his. Instead of finding anger, I find pleasure. He gives me a mischievous smirk, and his sky-blue eyes twinkle with a dark glint.

"Well, Tayla, you're everything I ever wanted." My heart stutters, and it stops for a second. Maybe longer. My head whirls with the words he uttered. I squirm and swig down the last bit of coffee.

"What do you mean?"

"Precisely what I said. I want you." Tension hovers in the air, and I stop breathing. Somehow, his words hold more than he said. "When can you start? I need someone used to the way we need things done before the tour. We have a month to get you up to speed." Everything rattles through my brain at a speed that takes me a while to catch up with. Foggy with confusion, desire, and pure adrenalin.

"Tomorrow." He nods.

"Be here at nine a.m. Do you need the car to pick you up?" *Did I?*

"I should be able to get here. My apartment isn't too far away." He nods again and offers me a mischievous smile.

"Good, that means you'll be on time. I hate when people are late. Let me walk you out." Standing on wobbly legs, his hand finds the small of my back as he guides me towards the stairs. As we descend, I have to hold onto the rail. I'm trembling from head to toe. That was one of the most intense conversations I've ever had. There's a crowd of people downstairs. We sidestep a few perched on the floor working on their laptops

"So, do I—"

"You will meet everyone tomorrow."

"Interrupting someone while they're talking is rude. It doesn't matter who you are." My retort earns me a chuckle, but I had to say something about it. His hand never leaves the spot on my back, and his touch sends my pulse skittering. The SUV is waiting for me once we reach the driveway. As I turn to face him, his hand drops. He reaches out and grasps my hand. His eyes never leaving mine. A smile curls his soft lips, and his tongue flicks out, moistening them. *Wow, that's hot! Ugh, Tayla, he's an asshole!*

"I promise never to interrupt you again." I nod. "Because the next time you see me, I will be your boss." He presents me with the sexiest smile. "And I expect you to obey my every word." *Who the fucking hell does he think he is?*

"You're very confident." His dark smirk is sexy as hell, and my core pulses. The sky-blue eyes that I have come to appreciate since I first saw him years ago on TV crease as he considers me with an amused expression. I should leave right now. This man is incredulous.

"I have to be. You got the job; let's see if you can handle the heat." He cocks his head to the side and stares right into my heart. It rattles me, and I avert my gaze immediately. Callum Hayes is going to be the death of me. This is a certainty. He was always the topic of conversation. Every girl I met through university freaked out whenever they saw him.

"Sure, I can." My eyes dart up to his, meeting him in challenge. "Question is, can you handle me?" *Where the fuck did that come from?* I guess I lost my mind. He is overly confident. Someone should take him down a notch. He has the bad-boy persona he portrays in the tabloids, but seeing him here, I don't believe it for a second. I'm almost certain he is the naughtier brother. One I should stay away from.

"Trust me, Tayla. I can handle everything you bring my way. We will see each other tomorrow." I pull my hand out of his grasp, not to be rude but because I can't think straight with him touching me.

I nod. "Tomorrow." He opens the back door, and I slip into the seat. His eyes are glazed with something that isn't professional, a scorching heat. He has me bewildered. My skin is tingling where he touched me. I need to be professional. I just got a job, a dream job. Looking down at my hands, I'm shaking. I inhale a deep breath as the car pulls out onto the street. The tension between us was so thick you could slice it with a knife. The heat he exuded was palpable. *How do I work with him?*

As soon as I step into my apartment, the tension in my muscles loosens. I landed a job working with the most incredible rock band. Making my way to the kitchen, I switch on the kettle and get my cup ready for a nice, strong coffee. The memory of spilling a cup of coffee over one of the hottest men in the world will haunt me forever. I should call Emma. I can just hear her freak out. She's loved Hunter since she was in high school. Tomorrow will be one interesting day. My life is about to change in a profound way.

Callum Hayes is challenging to work with; he's known as a perfectionist. And I don't doubt for a second I can learn a lot from the man. Although, deep down, I realize there's something else there. I felt it, and he did too. He's too old for me. Surely. I mean, he's thirty-five. That's seven years older. With his experience, he must be incredible in bed. I can't think like that though. Keeping it professional is what I should focus on.

I miss my sister right now. I have so much I want to tell her. To have her running into my bedroom talking a mile a minute would take my mind off Callum. She's the outgoing one, as I'm the cautious one. Maybe it's because she's younger by three years. I haven't been on a date in a year. The fear of what happened still haunts me. What he did will never go away. So, I avoid dates; it's easier. There is no explaining. If any man saw me naked, they would be appalled and run. My confidence couldn't take that. He made sure no man will come near me. That was his promise.

With the coffee made, I head into my living room and grab my laptop. Logging in to my user account, I open my Skype app. Emma isn't online yet. When we spoke last night, and I told her about the interview, she was thrilled. Now, when I tell her who the band is, I think she may pass out. With my mail app open, I scroll through all the spam, deleting as I go.

My Twitter account pops up, and Kierra has posted that they hired a new intern. My heart stutters against my rib cage. When I open another tab on my browser, I log into Hunter's online chat room and find a few hundred people there. It's a hangout for all the fans of the band.

They're chatting about the announcement. *Shit. Can I do this?* My attraction to him is undeniable. He's hot, sexy, and confident. He's bad news. Everyone knows Callum Hayes is the bad-boy rock star. I just need to keep it professional. It can't be that difficult. If anyone can do it, I can.

Most of my classmates from the university are big fans of Hunters in Oblivion. I know all their songs. There is a particular song that never fails to bring tears to my eyes. It's called "Damaged Angel." Their new album is doing well. With their tour only a month away, they have been teasing new songs online. It's like

Callum writes twenty-four hours a day. He loves to tease. Maybe that's why all the girls fall for him. It comes so naturally to him.

Scrolling down my Facebook timeline, I notice there are new photos of him in town wearing a T-shirt with the jeans he was wearing today. Groaning, I close my browser and leave my Skype open ready for my sister's call. *Can the attraction between us be a fluke?* I hope so because I want this job. More than I let on.

CALLUM

"Liam, get the rhythm right, please?" I'm frustrated. This morning replays in my mind on a continual loop. For the first time, I was challenged to the point of wanting to spank a girl for her insolence. She was beyond feisty. Her sassy little mouth with those soft pink, plump lips had me aching to drive my cock between them. The fact that she is so unaffected by me has me intrigued. No woman I have met since the band hit the big time has ever acted like I was just another guy. Tayla though, she is different. She's a mystery to me. I don't know how to handle a woman who doesn't throw herself at me. This is a challenge I won't mind taking. She looked incredible in that soft blue top. The thin spaghetti straps looked so delicate on her shoulders. Easy to rip off her magnificent body.

"Cal, what the fuck are you doing?" As I glance up, I realize everyone is staring at me. The Den where we are recording is filled with staff. My brother's inquisitive stare makes me uneasy. There is no way I am telling them about

Tayla. She's mine to have fun with. When Ki told me she was interviewing someone, a girl, I was intrigued. Initially, I wanted a guy to head up the sound, but Ki was adamant we needed more female staff on tour. So, I let her lead with the interviews, and I'm so glad I did. Since Tayla left, I've counted down the hours until I see that sweet little ass again. Her soft melodic voice sent blood straight to my cock. I would love to hear her moaning my name while I show her exactly what all the girls are always talking about — the devil inside my pants.

"Nothing. Working on the melody in my head." Brushing off his question, I get up and stalk to the kitchen. Ignoring the quips, I grab a bottle of water and gulp it down, anything to cool the fire burning me up from thoughts of her. I need to calm this raging fucking hard-on in my jeans.

"Callum, are you going to do a live feed today?" When I peer at Kierra, I can see the underlying question in her eyes. She knows me better than anyone. Working beside me for close to ten years, she's been my assistant and best friend. "What's going on with you, Cal?"

"Nothing. Why? Must there be something wrong with me? I am just thinking through things. I am not in the mood to go live today." She narrows her eyes at me. Knowing she will let it go puts me at ease. Although, it will be brought up again. That's what I am dreading. When she turns and walks away, I let out the breath I had been holding.

This girl is creating more shit than I thought she would. It makes no sense; she doesn't want me. Why do I want her? I can have any woman, in any country. But there is only one my sights are set on now, and she is my new sound engineer. It's going to be interesting having her here every day. Although, working with a hard-on will not be pleasant.

"Callum!" Fucking hell, do they have to make such a noise?

"I am coming! Don't fucking scream at me." Walking back into the Den, I see Liam is ready to go. Set up and the cameras are rolling. Did I not make myself clear, I don't want to do a live feed today? I sit down and grin into the lens. "Hey guys! What's everyone up to? Where are you from?" Kierra hands me the laptop, and the chat goes wild. There are people from all over. Girls in every corner of the globe, and they want me, Ryan, or my brother. Between the three of us, we have our own fan bases. I love lurking in the chat room occasionally, just to see what they talk about. There have been some downright dirty chats I've walked in on.

I created an online platform where our fans can chat, and I go online to say "hi." Being on the road, I haven't had a chance lately. Today is a first for a while. I am here, but my mind is elsewhere. "Okay, perverts, what's going on in here?" The messages fly by. There are now nine hundred people online. "Do you want me to take my top off?" The responses that come through after that are exactly what I expected. Dirty. I love to tease. It's what I do well. "Let's sing a song." Picking up my guitar, I strum a few chords and hum the tune to a favorite.

The lights twinkle below me. I love walking up here. The hillside behind my house is my private sanctuary. Only two other houses have access to it. Up here, I can think. There's an incredible peace, away from the noise, the screaming fans, and those goddamn drums of my brother's. I can't imagine living anywhere other than Los Angeles. I'm from a small town nobody has ever heard of. My brother and I grew up with nothing. Our mother taught us to work hard and believe in ourselves. She always gave as much as she could. That's why I learned to appreciate everything I have now; even the crazy fans. They are brazen, but they're loyal. That's why I give so much of myself. This — the fame, the popularity — can be taken away in a second. All I can do is enjoy it while it lasts.

As soon as I reach the top of the hill, those brown eyes pop into my mind. She's so beautiful. There's something about her though, a wariness. I want to break down that barrier and discover what's inside. To see into her heart, find her passion, and unleash it. She's tiny, a mere five-foot-four to my five-foot-eight, and her sleek, ice-blonde hair flows down her back. Long enough for me to wrap around my fist while I have her bent over. Those chestnut eyes seem to bore into me. More profound than anyone has ever seen. She sees past the façade. That terrifies me, but it also excites me. Never has a girl challenged me like Tayla. Her retort was adorable. They normally just nod and giggle. Always hanging on my every fucking word. Sometimes, it's just nice to be around someone who acts normal around me. Gives me a run for my money, so to speak.

I'm not normal, I suppose. The public call me many things; normal isn't one of them. My brother doesn't deal with fame as I do. He's been through a lot. So have I, but I can block it out. He can't. I used to do things I'm not proud of. I've used women and abused alcohol. I was the asshole everyone said I was. At thirty-five, I guess I've grown up. Being in this industry will jade you. I'm no longer the asshole, but most people don't know that. Only a handful of my closest friends know the real me, and that's how I want it.

Making my way back to the house, I take deep, calming breaths. There's a fucking song that's been pestering me, and I need to write. Music has been a constant in my life. Something I could turn to when I was feeling depressed. When the impulse to take drugs again reared its ugly fucking head. There are so many occasions I made it through using music.

As soon as I step inside, I hear the drums. God, isn't he sleeping yet? There is only one place I want to be right now. Once I'm in my refuge, I close the bedroom door and flop down on my bed. Closing my eyes, I count slowly, one through ten and back. Chestnut eyes invade my mind again. *Fuck this!* My eyes snap open. Hopping off the bed, I head next door to the music room. The piano sits snuggly in the corner. Just what I need to forget her, but it's impossible. Her scent is still in the room. Sitting on the stool, I tap the ivories. The melody in my head that's been driving me crazy since yesterday plays through me onto the keys. Once she left, I came in here. Sat at the piano waiting on the muse in my mind's eye. Nothing concrete came, but my thoughts were busy. Creating. It's those brown eyes. No woman has affected me like she has, not since my ex. A shiver runs down my spine— an icy, disgusted shiver.

I was so in love, but she broke me. No other word explains it better. She shattered anything I had built with her. When I realized she was using me for my fame, I walked. Not looking back. Never again will anyone do that to me. That's why I put so much into my music. I can't afford to lose it over a woman. So, I play the asshole. The bad boy everyone thinks I am.

I'm sitting in the office when my assistant

walks in. "Hey, Ki, we have to complete the contract for Tayla." I glance up at my assistant and grin. She knows employing a new girl will give her some semblance of gaining a friend — someone to talk to when all the guys are too much to handle. I keep my staff busy. Perfection. It's the control I need to make sure my life is on track. Some people think I work too hard, but I can sleep when I am dead, right?

"Cal, I know you. Can you tell me what the hell is going on with you?" Her piercing blue eyes stare a hole into me. They're not as blue as mine. They're a stormy grey with hints of blue depending on her mood. She always does this. Shaking my head, I shrug. "Don't give me that shit." She's a dainty little stick of dynamite. Not taking shit from anyone, including me. That's why I hired her.

"There's nothing wrong. Get off my back, woman."

"Bullshit! You've been weird since the interview this morning. Even when you were doing the stream earlier, you looked like you weren't even here. You think they don't notice when you're not yourself?" Her question has me putting my guard up. I wish she would give this a rest. There is nothing wrong.

"Kierra, I am myself. I sang, teased them. Asked them to buy merch. What else do you want from me?" As soon as the words are out of my mouth, I know she will blow. Her face is stone.

"We need this intern. If you didn't like her, then why did you agree? She's starting tomorrow, and now you're all screwed up in the head again. I hope you will sort your shit out before she arrives. With the tour coming up, we can't afford—"

"Fuck, Kierra! Just give it a rest. I know what I'm doing. Don't tell me how to run my life!" Stalking out of the office, I slam the door behind me. *Shit*. That was uncalled for, but I don't care right now. I reach the patio and step outside and take a deep breath. The click of her heels on the tiles alerts me that she's followed me.

"Callum Hayes, if you ever speak to me like that again, I will walk out. Do you hear me?" I nod. Nothing I can say will make it better. Yes, I was wrong. Maybe an apology will suffice.

"Sorry." When I don't turn to her, she rounds on me, and her penetrating stare forces me to look at her. "What? I can't say anything else. There's nothing more you need to know."

"Right. So Tayla?" I gape at my assistant. How the fuck did she do that?

"I don't understand what you're talking about."

"Bullshit, Cal! The last time you were so . . ." She waves her hand in the air, trying to find the words. I stay silent, waiting for her to finish her tirade. "Fucked in the head was when you were with Arina."

My glare is deadly. "Do not, ever, mention her name again. She has no fucking right even to be thought about. There is nothing you need to know. So, give it up, Kierra. I would appreciate it if you did not mention my ex again. Just go home. You're here late again." She sighs loudly, and I realize she's giving up. Finally.

"Fine, but Callum, when you finally talk to this girl again, be nice." She spins on her heel and walks back into the house with me staring after her. There isn't a way for me to convince her there isn't a girl because there is a girl — one with chestnut eyes and shiny blonde hair. With beautiful curves and a set of tits, I want to bury my cock between. Great, now I have a fucking hard-on!

As I said, Tayla will be the death of me.

I have been sitting here for hours. Kierra left two hours ago, and I'm still nowhere near finding the lyrics that evade me. How am I meant to get songs done for an album when my mind can't relax? This tour will take a lot out of me. There is pressure on us with the amount of work that goes into a worldwide tour. It's astonishing. Tomorrow is Tayla's first day. I gave Kierra a list of things I want Tay to learn. She needs to be up to scratch for the upcoming tour.

Since Ki will handle her first day, I can stay away, which is what I need to do. If I went down there, I would give her too much to handle. There is *something* I want her to handle. Thoughts of her soft hands on my cock have me straining against my zipper. Me being famous didn't faze her, and she's just as jaded by the LA lifestyle. Maybe I can wine and dine her. If that will get me into her little panties, then I'm all for it. I always give one hundred percent.

I can be as romantic as she wants. Glancing at the sheet in front of me — the empty fucking sheet — I wince. This will be a painful process. The label will lose their shit when they know we only have one song, and it's not even finished. In fact, it's far from finished. I unlock my phone and scroll through my contacts. I need a distraction. It's late, and I know a perfect little brunette who will take my mind off this shit.

"Hello?" Her voice is soft and sweet as she whispers into the phone.

"Hey, kitten, can I come play?" Her giggle is answer enough. She didn't realize it's me since I never give my number to anyone. I don't need fucking stalkers hounding me.

"Callum." She breaths my name, seductively. "Yes, come over." As soon as I hang up, I pull on my black boots and make my way out to the garage. It's only hit midnight. I can be home before the sun rises. She doesn't live too far away — one of my many contacts. Girls ready to take the edge off but never wanting more.

When I reach her apartment, it's quiet, and no lights are on. Once I step up to her door, before I even have a chance to knock, she's swinging the door open and jumping into my arms.

"I missed you." She stares at me. Her words are too tender. There's feeling in them, and I need to stop that immediately.

"I want a fuck, kitten. Nothing more." Yes, I am a dick, but she knew what she was signing up for when she agreed. I walk us back into the apartment. My mouth on hers, she opens easily. So eager. I lick into her. Tasting her. The little whimpers from her mouth are soft as my tongue dances with hers. She sucks on it like a porn star, and who knows? She could be. I don't get to know them.

Our hands are everywhere, yanking and tugging at clothes until we're both naked. Her tight body is sexy — no scars, no ink, just soft, smooth skin. So beautiful. For tonight. To be honest, I love girls with ink. But kitten here, she's pure. Unmarked.

Lifting her up by her ass, I throw her back onto the bed, and she giggles as her long, brown hair fans around her on the pillow. "Open your legs. Touch your little pussy." She loves putting on a show, and it makes me fucking hard. Her smooth, bare cunt spread for me. She's already glistening, and I can't wait to sink into her. I reach for my jeans strewn on the floor and pull out a condom. Tearing the wrapper, I sheath myself. Her gaze is locked on my movements, and she moans at the sight.

"You're so big, Cal." *I know that kitten, that's why you will scream when I fuck your tight little body.* Kneeling between her legs, I slowly tease her with the tip of my cock.

"Ready for me, kitten?" She nods. The hungry gaze she locks on me has me raging. Without warning, I thrust into her, balls-deep in her tight pussy. Fuck, it feels so good. Her head falls back, and her eyes flutter closed as I pound her into the bed. She wraps her legs around my waist, pulling me in deeper. My mouth finds her pebbled nipple, and I suck on it. I bite down just enough to give her a jolt of pleasured pain, and she cries out. Her tight heat is pulsing, and she's close. I pull out almost all the way to the tip and slam into her, bottoming out as she screams my name. Her orgasm takes hold of her. I drive in again and again. On the third thrust, I fill the rubber. Once she's come down from her high, I slip out of her and get dressed. By the time I reach the door, she's followed me into the living room, wrapped in a sheet.

"You're not staying?" She's getting needy. I don't like it.

"I never do. You know that." The sorrow in her green stare only makes me want to run faster. Once I'm in the safety of my Jeep, I sigh. Pulling out my phone, I scroll to her number and delete it. There is no way I am getting into this again. As I start the car, there's no satisfaction in what I did. My body is on edge. There's only one girl who can sate me. One with blonde hair and brown eyes.

TAYLA

The sound of my alarm pulls me from the anxiety, but something was unusual this time. Nightmares have haunted me for three years. Or rather, he has plagued me. Today, I can't let that get to me. There's something to look forward to. My future. It's my first day of work with Hunters in Oblivion. I'm bummed I couldn't talk to my sister last night, but she did text and let me know she'll be online tonight. Well, her morning. She had a deadline and needed to complete her assignment.

Rolling over in bed, I stare up at the ceiling. I'll be on tour with one of my favorite bands on their upcoming Lust & Temptation tour. The album of the same name was only released six months ago. And I had it on repeat every day. Actually, I had one song on replay. "Damaged Angel." Something about the crack in Callum's voice as he reaches the chorus makes my heart race. I'm the damaged angel. At least that's how I feel. When he sings it, it's as if he's speaking directly to me. Remembering his intense blue stare has my skin tingling and goosebumps rising over my body. It would be a lie to deny he does things to me. My thighs squeeze together instinctively. *Doesn't every girl do that when they think of him?* He's taller than me by a few inches. His beautifully sculpted jaw was dusted with stubble. He has a toned torso I would love to run my tongue along. The man is beautiful. Plain and simple.

The prospect of spending time around him has the butterflies fluttering in my stomach. *How can I deny that I want him?* I can't. That's my problem. But if working with them means I get to travel and gain experience, I'm all for it.

My crew access will be VIP. Backstage passes to see the craziness that ensues before shows and after. It would be a twenty-four-hour responsibility. Kierra said it's going to be intense, hard work, but that doesn't intimidate me. That excites me — an experience of a lifetime. One I'm looking forward to. The only problem will be staying as far away from Callum as possible. I shouldn't let my attraction to him mess up my chance at a career in this industry. Did I have to land a job with the hottest rock stars in the world?

Since I will be spending most of my time with the crew, I won't need to talk to him at all. So, this will be easier than I expect. *So, why does it still make me so nervous?*

At least Kierra seems nice. She's been photographed with Cal since I've been a fan of the band. From the photographs taken of her, she always comes across as serious. Since the guys are always so goofy, most reporters enjoy talking to them. They love having a laugh, and watching them in interviews online is hilarious.

There were always rumors that Kierra and Cal were dating but never any proof. I mean, working alongside one of the hottest rock stars in the world, there must be an attraction? Some of the comments I read in the chat room used to make me blush. I wonder if he ever sees what they say about him? He probably enjoys the attention.

Rolling out of bed, I pad to the kitchen and turn on my beloved kettle. Today, caffeine will be my best friend. Turning on the sound system in the living room, I'm startled by Callum's voice singing about "Filthy Lust." The video for this song is one for late-night viewing. He always goes all out. I remember my sister practically melting on our sofa when it was released. Callum wears next to nothing in the video. There is a scene of him stepping out of the shower, which I must admit has me drooling. I wonder if his abs are that defined?

What are you thinking? Shaking my head, I make my way to the bathroom. I can't be thinking of Callum. Not right now.

Stepping out of the shower, I groan in

frustration when I take in my appearance. The black circles under my eyes from not sleeping properly are noticeable. As soon as I open my closet, another groan escapes my lips. What the hell do I wear? Something professional but sexy. I want to make a good impression on the band. The thought of meeting the rest of the guys has butterflies waking in my belly. As much as I want to deny it, I know seeing those cerulean eyes will be my undoing.

I need to focus on work. This is my area of expertise. I know how to do this. Inhaling a deep breath, I calm myself and grab a pair of skinny jeans. They're dark blue, so they look dressy. I opt for a white, slouchy tee, which has a massive cherry blossom flower on the front. It's comfortable but pretty. It falls off one shoulder and isn't too low cut. If I will be running around and working with instruments, I don't want to dress up.

The upcoming tour will be incredible. With this being their fourth album, it's already selling millions of copies. Now all I need is to get up to speed on how they like their instruments set up, and I will be fine. Let's just hope the month before the tour will pass by quickly. Once we step on the plane, I can relax. I will most likely spend all my time with the crew, so my distraction with Callum can take a backseat.

My phone beeps showing a new message. Unlocking the screen, I open the text and smile. It's my sister, and she has news. It can only mean she met someone. That's normally why she'd freak out and get excited. We are two sides of a coin. Her hair is brown and hangs in long waves, and her elegant dress sense is opposite to my more boyish one. She has green eyes, whereas mine are brown.

E: Hiya babe, I miss your boring ass! Can we Skype later? I have fucking incredible news!! xo

We definitely need to chat. I have to tell her about my new job. I hit the reply button.

T: Yes! I have something exciting to tell you too xo

My legs take me up the hill to the house. I have my coffee in hand, ready to start the day. When I reach the driveway, there's a black Suzuki motorcycle parked outside. It's gorgeous and shiny; I recognize it immediately. It's Liam's. He rode this bike in one of their music videos. I'm still staring at the incredible machine when the gate flies open, and I come face to face with caramel eyes. Wow! The other Hayes brother is taller by a few inches. He has broad shoulders, and his tanned skin looks soft and smooth. "Well, hello there, little one. Are you lost?" Immediately, I recognize that low, gravelly voice from interviews.

"No, I . . . My name is Tayla. I'm the new intern." I offer my hand. For a moment, I think he's only going to stare at me. Then he takes it, and his rough, callused fingers feel so different from Callum's. A drummer's hands. We shake slowly, and the muscles in his forearm flex, and I'm mesmerized. Both brothers are put together in flawless perfection. Their parents did a good job producing them.

"My brother has good taste in staff." The wicked gleam in his eyes tells me there's way too much underlying that comment. A blush spreads over my cheeks. His hungry, caramel gaze rakes over me, taking in every inch of my appearance before landing on my face.

"Thank you. I guess I better get inside." He nods. Releasing my hand and walks past me.

"I will see more of you later, sweet cheeks." He pulls on his helmet and swings his leg over the bike. He's rough, sexy, and the complete opposite of his brother.

I walk up to the house, still reeling from my meeting with the eldest Hayes. With a quick glance, I find a few staff sitting on the patio. They offer me a small smile as I step inside. Kierra comes flying out of an office. "Yay! You're here." She tugs me by the hand and pulls me into the kitchen. "Do you want coffee?" I take in the massive kitchen.

"I have one." Lifting my cup. "This is incredible." My eyes dart toward her and gesture around the room that looks more like it belongs on a movie set. She giggles at my expression.

"Wait till you see the rest of the house. You ready to get started?" I nod and smile. We take a quick tour of the offices, the studio, and she shows me where the restroom is. The house is bigger than I thought. From the outside, it looks small. There are so many hidden rooms and closets.

We head back to the office to go over my contract. It's a six-month internship. Afterward, I have an option to extend it and become a permanent member of the staff, or I can leave.

"I need you to read through everything. There are a number of clauses. You cannot talk about anything that takes place here whether it's with friends and family or press. Everything you will hear and see is confidential. We need to trust our staff. If anything is leaked, we will investigate. If you're found guilty, it's immediate termination." I nod. This is expected. She leaves me then, and I sit back, reading through the thick document.

My skin prickles and I feel him before he speaks. The intensity of his aura surrounds him like a cloud, and my body responds. My glance flits up, and I'm met with cerulean eyes. "Good morning, Callum." I smile and make to get up.

"Tayla." The way my name rolls off his tongue is erotic. Already I'm squirming. This is ridiculous. His hand extends, and when I slip mine in his, a spark shoots from my fingertips right down to my toes. This man exudes sex.

He's dressed in a pair of blue jeans. They're ripped at the knees, and he's wearing slippers. The black T-shirt that molds to every contour of his lean, muscular chest has me involuntarily licking my lips.

"How are you?" My voice comes out thick with emotion. Desire. Yearning. Need.

"Better now. Are you happy with the contract?" His gaze falls on the desk. My hand is still in his, but he makes no move to release it.

"Yes, thank you. Six months will make a huge difference, giving me the experience I need. I hope to extend it." A smile tugs at the corner of his mouth, and he takes a step toward me. He leans in, and my breathing stops. *Is he going to kiss me?* His mouth is at my ear, and his hot breath fans over my neck, sending a shiver of lust down my spine and tingles straight to my clit.

"If you can handle six months with me, then you're unquestionably getting an extension." When he steps back, he drops my hand and turns to walk out of the office. Before he disappears, he pauses, facing me again. "And Tayla, you look beautiful." His hungry eyes rake over me, from my head to my tennis shoes. The heat that follows his gaze over my skin has me squirming. With that, he's gone.

It's almost lunchtime when Kierra walks

into the editing studio to find me. I have been sitting with the video editors learning about the process of getting a music video from raw footage to the final product. "You hungry, doll?" I smile and nod. "Come on, let's get something to eat. We can chat."

We make our way downstairs, and she is talking a mile a minute. I think she's so excited to have someone to chat with that she doesn't realize she's doing it.

"So, when are the guys recording?"

"Callum is busy writing every day. He works on the melodies, using the piano or his laptop. He hands it to Liam and Ryan to work through. They add in their parts, and then if Cal has the lyrics ready, they sit down and record. It's a long process. One song could take two weeks, maybe more to get to a place where Callum is happy."

"My brother is never happy." A deep rumble behind me has me jumping. I turn and come face to face with Liam.

"Liam, please don't start. Your brother is in a mood today."

"He's always in a mood." He turns and smiles. "You'll get used to it." Heading to the coffee machine, he grabs a mug and fills it.

"Anyway. Do you eat meat?" She stares at me, and I nod.

"Yes, I do." Seeming happy, she turns and continues plating food and pops it into the microwave. "And you?"

"Yes, sometimes. I end up just eating meat

at home. Since Callum doesn't, I tend to forget about it. It's second nature now." She smiles, handing me the plate of stir-fry. It smells incredible. "He made this yesterday. Sorry about the leftovers, but I promise it's good." I'm still aware of Liam watching us.

"Right, girls, I need to go bang . . . some drums." He flashes me a wolfish grin and winks as he makes his way out of the kitchen.

"He can be such an ass." She laughs and shakes her head. The rumors must be true. Liam has been seen photographed with countless beautiful women on his arm. Then again, so has Callum. *Who am I kidding?* Cal is in a league of his own. I have seen the women he dates, and they're a far cry from me.

"Do either of them have a girlfriend?" Her laugh is loud, and I suddenly feel self-conscious for asking.

"No, doll. They're both single. Liam will never settle down. At least that's what I think. Callum, he's different. He plays the bad boy, but he's actually a sweetheart. The girl that steals his heart will be one lucky bitch." She glances at me, and her mouth curls in an easy grin. "He's like my big brother. I want him happy. Both of them, for that matter."

"I always thought you and Callum were dating. Most of the fans do."

"Oh, God no. I could never date him. That would be weird. There is no way I can handle Callum Hayes. He's a nightmare at the best of times." We both collapse in a fit of giggles. I like her. She's honest, sweet, and I feel at ease with her.

We finish up our lunch in relaxed silence, and she takes me into the studio. We find Ryan with his keyboard; he looks so happy. Almost as if he is smiling at himself. He glances up as we enter and offers me a face-splitting grin. "Hello. I'm Ryan." We shake hands.

"Tayla. The newbie."

"Welcome."

"Ryan, can you show Tay the sound stuff?" She waves her hand around, and he chuckles. "That's my technical term for all this." Kierra normally handles the paperwork. And her so-called technical term has me giggling again. The look that passes between them is distinct. The way she looks at Ryan is filled with more emotion than when she looks at the other guys.

"Sure. Leave us to it. She'll be a pro in no time." When he offers her a wink, her blush is unmistakable. There's chemistry between them, and I can't help grinning. It's adorable. Kierra leaves us.

"So, darling. What are we doing today? Have you worked on a sound desk?"

"Only at college. I used to help out where I could."

"Cool, grab a seat. Let's work on this track. I laid down keyboards on Liam's drums. It's a newer track, so you won't recognize it." He presses a few buttons, and a sound wave pops up onscreen. The drums thump from the speakers mounted on the walls. It's so intense. The keyboards come in a few beats later, and the song comes to life. The only thing missing is the vocals.

"Wow. That's incredible." We glance at each other, and he nods. We spend the next hour just mixing and changing the different dials on the desk around. My brain feels fuzzy by the time Callum walks into the studio. His heated blue gaze flits between Ryan and me. We're sitting right next to each other, and I can tell Callum isn't happy about it. I frown and narrow my eyes, taking in his reaction. As soon as it appears, it's gone a second later.

"Ryan, can you give Tayla and me a sec? I want to chat with her before she leaves for the day." Ryan nods, gives me a smile and walks to the door.

"See you tomorrow, darling." With a quick wink, he's gone. My skin prickles. I am too aware of Callum and me alone in the studio. The heat emanating from his body is primal. The fire in his eyes turns me to molten lava.

"You have a good day?" His whisper is low. The dirty smirk that curls his lips has my core tightening and butterflies are fluttering in my belly. *Get a grip, Tay!*

"Yes, it's been good. I've learned a lot." He pulls up a chair and sits next to me. Ice-blue orbs scorching me as they search my eyes for something, although I'm sure what.

"So, who do you prefer?" His question is serious. The inflection in his voice is a deep rumble. Intensity burns in his gaze, and it consumes me. Piercing a hole straight through me. The fans have always been split between the guys. There are the girls who are team Callum, team Liam, or team Ryan. You can't be on all three. You have to choose one. With a grin on my lips, I decide to test his patience.

"I prefer the drummer." My gaze locks on his and the irritation in his eyes is palpable.

"Let me change your preference? Go to dinner with me?" My mouth drops open, and I stare at him. Callum leans forward, his face inches from mine. The warmth of his breath fans over my face, and my brain short circuits. I need to stop this right here. *What? Dinner? A date with Callum Hayes?*

"Callum, I can't." His fingers trail up my arm to my shoulder, tracing the intricate tattoo of cherry blossoms and vines. The heat of his fingertips on my exposed skin sends shockwaves through me, and my skin prickles with excitement. He leans in farther, his intoxicating scent enveloping me and holding me hostage.

"Say yes." It's so soft I think I imagine him talking.

"It's not a good idea." My voice is a whisper. Determination in his expression tells me he won't take no for an answer. Those blue pools darken with a fire that matches the one in my belly.

"Why? It's only dinner. I'll be a gentleman. Do you trust me?" There's something in his gaze that makes me want to nod. To tell him I would love to go to dinner with him, but he *will* hurt me. He's Callum fucking Hayes.

"I don't know you well enough to trust you." Our eyes lock in a standoff, and I forget to breathe. "Yet." The word is a mere whisper, and uncertainty flickers across his gaze. He's so close. The spicy scent of him grips me, keeping me in a warm cocoon. *Can I be with a rock star? Someone whose constantly in the public eye?*

"Then give me a chance to show you that you can trust me. You have nothing to lose. And so much to gain." Clarity sinks in, and I suppose he's right. I am not promising my heart or love. It's just dinner. Then we can go on with our lives. "Are you scared?" His questioning gaze challenges me.

A laugh so soft falls from my lips. "I'm not scared. That's for sure." He really has a high opinion about himself. There's a challenge hanging in the air, and I won't back down. *Is it such a bad idea? Yes!* My stubbornness doesn't allow me to back down. "Fine. I'll go. To prove I'm different from other women. I'm not falling to my knees for you." As soon as the words slip from my mouth, the fire in his eyes lights with desire. I realize how that sounded, and I cringe inwardly.

"Tayla, I know you're not like any other woman. That's why I'm asking. Once I break down those high walls you have built up around you, Petal, I look forward to seeing the treasure they keep hidden." With a naughty wink, he rises, and I immediately miss the heat of him. "And as for you on your knees, let's just say I can't wait to see that." I offer him a glare but don't give in to the dig. I rise and follow him out of the office.

The living room is quiet; everyone must have left. I grab my bag and make my way to the patio. Liam and Ryan are sitting back with a beer each while Kierra is on a call, and she offers me a wave.

"Bye, darling. See you tomorrow." Ryan holds up his hand to fist pump mine. I laugh at his chilled-out demeanor. I glance at Liam, and I catch his hungry eyes staring at me like I'm dinner.

"Tayla, tomorrow you're all mine. I need to show you how to set up my drums." I nod and offer a small grin.

"Come on, I'll walk you out." Callum's hand drops to my lower back, and goosebumps rise over my body. We wander up to the driveway, and click the remote on my key fob, unlocking the car door. I turn to him and smile.

"Thank you for this opportunity. The job. It means a lot."

"Anytime, beautiful. I look forward to dinner." With a tender caress on my cheek, his fingertips leave a trail of fire on my skin. My heart flutters at the statement. It's only dinner.

47

How bad can that be?

"Me too." He opens the door, and I slip into the driver's seat. He shuts me in, and I start the engine. When I pull away, I can't help but glance in the rear view mirror to find him standing on the sidewalk until I'm far down the road. I'm left speechless and confused. *I am so fucked.*

CALLUM

As soon as I step inside the house, Liam rounds on me. He noticed my hand on her back. The air is thick with emotion between Tayla and me. Everyone noticed. Ki is not naïve; she scowls at me, and I know why. I don't blame her. *I am so fucked.* "What the hell was that?" His tone is sharp, and my glare falls on him. I am not in the mood for this.

"What do you mean?"

"Jesus, Cal, I'm not fucking blind. You just about jumped her bones out there." I groan. Turning around, I walk into the studio. I can feel my brother behind me.

"It's nothing. Let it go." Grabbing my guitar, I sit down. There is no way I'm meeting his gaze. He'll see right through me. "Please?"

"Jesus, you're a sucker for punishment. Fine. Just be careful. You realize you can't be with this woman. She's our intern. The fucking papers will have a field day." There isn't anything I can do. Doesn't he understand that? She's in my fucking head.

"Liam, I realize that. I am not a fucking idiot." Without another word, he spins on his heel and saunters out. Leaving me to my never-ending thoughts of a woman. I asked her to dinner. That's not something I normally do, but something about her makes me want to know her. My fingers strum the chords of a melody that's been playing in my mind for the past few days. It's slow, soft, different from my other songs.

"Cal, can we sort this contract out? You added a clause?"

"Yes." I peer up at Kierra as she walks into the room. There's something she wants to say. I know it.

"And the point of this is?"

"Kierra, forget this. What the fuck is wrong with everyone? I need to be on my own." Before she can answer, I place my guitar down, stand up, and walk past my assistant to the door.

"I know what you're doing, Cal. I suggest you stop whatever little plan you're formulating in your head." My hand twists the door handle. Not turning to Kierra, I open it and walk out. Pulling out my phone, I call my mother. She'll give me advice. I'm out of my comfort zone here. Unfortunately, I get her voicemail. On the patio, I glance around. The staff has all left, and it's quiet. My favorite time of day and when I have a few minutes alone. *"Liam Hayes!"* Kierra's scream has me chuckling. My brother is always in trouble. Shaking my head, I walk up to the gate and slip out. Maybe a walk will do me good. With my phone in hand, I update my social media status and check the updates. Two hundred notifications that I don't want to think about. We're announcing our new tour in two days, and that's when the madness starts.

When I reach the boulder at the top of the hill, I sit back and scroll through the contacts. Her number is there. I save all my crew's numbers. *Will a message be too personal?* I know what she thinks. She's seen the tabloids. What can I say? I can be a party animal. Even though I have done things I shouldn't, in public, I wouldn't do that with her. There is something different about Tayla. Something tells me this woman will be a challenge. My eyes flit up to the view in front of me. A city that made my dreams a reality. The City of Angels. That's where I got the title for our hit single, "Damaged Angel." This is the land of dreams, where they're created and destroyed. I open the message app. She might not reply, but I might as well try.

C: What's your favorite food?

I hit send and sit back, watching the sun disappear behind the horizon. The tranquil atmosphere calms me somewhat. A few minutes later, my phone buzzes. Sliding the unlock screen, I see her name pop up. Before I open the message, I take a deep breath. My heart is racing against my chest. It's an unusual feeling, wanting and needing someone to talk to you. I'm so used to people vying for my attention Tayla confounds me. She's not like the other women. There isn't an inkling in her actions to tell me she is impressed by my fame.

T: Callum? If you're asking my favorite food to try and impress me tomorrow, then I consider that cheating. Remember, this is dinner, not a date.

I can't help chuckling at her response. She's right. I am trying to impress her. Why? I have no fucking clue, but I want to.

C: Fine, I will cook. Then you will be impressed.

Once I hit send, I immediately see the dots on my screen. She's obviously in the mood for banter, and to be honest, so am I.

T: I don't trust your cooking. I would much rather go to a drive-thru.

C: LOL! No, Petal, it's not healthy to eat that shit. I have never eaten at one. Ever. So you will have to trust my choice in a restaurant.

As soon as I hit send, I realize I called her doll face. *Shit!* She will call me out on it, and I won't be able to explain myself. At least, not unless I want a slap. I can't help it if her face is perfect. She doesn't need tons of makeup. She's a natural beauty. The other thing I couldn't help noticing was her perfect-peach ass. Fuck, I definitely want a bite of that. I bet she tastes as sweet.

T: Petal? Seriously? Do you call all your staff strange names? I think I trust your taste in food, since you're vegetarian.

She's obviously done her research. I have been vegetarian for years, so she will have to trust me. I hit reply and chuckle.

C: Yes, I have nicknames for all my staff, as a matter of fact, and yours happens to be Petal. Yes, I am vegetarian. Aren't you an intelligent woman. Been googling me?

I don't have to wait long for her reply.

T: Sure you do. I haven't been googling. To be honest, I'm a fan. Since I was about fifteen. So is my sister.

Interesting. Okay, that will make this easier. She will be in my bed sooner than I thought. I'll make sure her fandom status only grows, much like my cock at the image of having her pink, plump lips wrapped around it. Her beautiful brown eyes looking up at me, sparkling while I fuck her pretty face. I need to stop this. I can't walk back to the house with a raging fucking hard-on.

C: Well, that makes this so much more interesting. See you tomorrow, doll face, and behave yourself. If you don't, take pics and send them to me ;)

With that, I make my way down the hill. It's dark now, and I hope Liam has called it a night. I want to relax and think about where I'll take the lovely Tayla. This will be interesting, for sure. As I step into the house, there isn't a soul in sight. The lights are off, and I walk into the kitchen, grabbing a bottle of chilled water from the fridge. My phone buzzes and I pull it from my pocket.

T: In your dreams, Hayes. :)

Yes, in my dreams. That's precisely where you will be tonight. I grab a towel from my bedroom and walk into the *en suite* bathroom. I love my space. It's the only thing that keeps me mildly relaxed in the chaos that's our home office. Since we've been doing all our recording and filming here, it's been chaos. I can't wait to get on the road again. Stepping into the hot spray, I feel my muscles relax. *Tayla Quinn is going to dinner with me.*

I'll prove to her I'm not the asshole the tabloids make me out to be. There's only one problem. Will she finally believe me? I wonder if she would consider dating. If not, I can make sure she can't get enough of me. I will have this girl. Once the water cools, I step out and towel dry myself. In the bedroom, I find my phone vibrating on the nightstand. I slide my finger over the unlock screen and find a message. It's her.

T: *You sleeping already?*

C: *No, did you miss me? I just got out of the shower. Want a pic?*

T: *Don't be an ass, Callum Hayes. I actually need to sleep tonight, no nightmares.*

I can't help wondering what nightmares she has. But then the emoji she's added after the message makes my mind wander. *Is she flirting?* I think she's flirting. *Fuck yes.* I knew she couldn't withstand my irresistible charm. And of course, all the girls know I'm packing a monster. That's why they want me, for recognition of fucking a rock star so they can climb the ladder. I'm not complaining. As much as I want her in my bed, I have a feeling this is different from my regular hookups. This will not be one night. And that scares the shit out of me. But I want to see how far she's willing to go.

C: *Doll face, if you've seen what I am hiding, you wouldn't want to sleep.*

T: *Goodnight, Hayes, I will see you tomorrow.*

C: *Sweet dreams, doll face. xo*

I love how she's let down her guard with me. She seems more relaxed. I wonder how long that will last. So far, step one is complete. Flopping onto my king-sized bed, I can't stop imagining her blonde hair splayed on my pillow. Against the soft black cotton sheets, her skin like ivory in contrast to the ebony. Imagining her moaning my name in that sweet sexy voice has me hard as a rock. I want to be inside her tight little body. To feel her tighten around me. She will be under me, in my bed, very fucking soon.

"Callum fucking Hayes, that's what you'll be screaming darling." My gaze falls on a beautiful brunette who just walked in. We just finished the show, and my brother disappeared with a girl, actually two, and I know he won't be coming back soon. He always does this. After every show, a few girls are always ready and waiting, and he takes full advantage. Me, I'm picky.

Don't get me wrong, I take advantage of these women. The ache to get my cock squeezed by a tight pussy is always there. The adrenaline after finishing a show has my blood pumping. Now there's a cute little brunette with a sexy body staring up at me with big doe eyes. All I can think of is burying myself in her for an hour or two.

I pull her into my room. When the door shuts, she's on me like she's climbing a fucking tree. Hungry little whimpers escape her plump lips. This isn't how

I do things, darling. I am in charge. *I push her until she's kneeling before me. "This is how I want you . . . for now." A wink and she's giggling. She knows what's coming.*

With my jeans at my knees, I tug my boxer briefs down. Her gaze falls on my hard, thick cock. "Will you be able to take every inch in your pretty little mouth, kitten?"

"Yes." Her eyes are round in . . . Shock? Awe? I don't know or care.

"Open your mouth, tongue out." My voice is thick with lust. She complies sweetly. Fisting her long brown hair, I bring her to my dick. Sinking into her warm, wet mouth is heaven, and my head drops back. Not stopping, I thrust until I hit the back of her throat. The sound of her choking spurs me on, and with a wicked grin, I push just a little more. Fuck, that feels good. *Her tiny hands come up and grip my thighs.*

I glance down and find her beautiful eyes shining with tears. When I slide out, she smiles. "You like that, little one?" I watch her lick her lips, and that's all I needed as I fuck her mouth. Faster and deeper. She takes me, but not all nine inches. No girl can take it all as her jaw will be sore later. Her whimpering and moaning around my dick has my release shooting down my spine, and my balls tighten. "You want rock star seed, slut?" She nods enthusiastically. And that's when I give it to her — every fucking drop.

My eyes snap open. The dreams and memories assault my sleep. Every night, it's like I can't escape my past. Swinging my feet over the side of the bed, I glance at the alarm clock.

It's only seven a.m., but I know most of my staff will mill around the house. Today is my date with Tayla. Since it's at six p.m., I have to think about where we should go. Grabbing a pair of sweatpants, I pull them on and walk into the living room. Just as I thought, it's buzzing with staff. "Mr. Hayes." My newest web designer is in early. We're launching our new website, and I want everything working perfectly.

"Christopher, is everything ready? It needs to go live at midday."

"Yes, I have it ready. I'm testing everything again, and I'll set it up for midday launch." Nodding, I make my way to the kitchen. I need coffee. As soon as I step into the room, I come face to face with chestnut eyes. Fuck, she looks incredible today. She's just filled a mug. Her gaze travels over my bare chest and slowly down to my waist. Like she's reading a book, I notice her take in every inch of the ink on my ribs. There is hunger in her eyes, and I allow her to take her fill.

"Callum, how are you today?" I don't have to turn to my assistant. She's oblivious to Tayla, and I locked in a battle devouring each other. Tay looks like a kitten ready to pounce on her toy. I wouldn't mind being that toy.

"Kierra, are we finished with the schedule for the tour? Everything must be confirmed before the end of the week. I want our team to get together one night. Everyone needs a copy of the requirements, venues, and timing." I don't move my gaze from the blonde bombshell in my kitchen, dressed in a white skirt, which stops above her knee. The material looks soft, silky. Her top is sheer black, and under she's wearing one of the tank tops from our merchandise store. It's tight and fits her perfectly. Showing off curves and tits. I would give anything to lift that little skirt and find out what panties she's wearing. A quick tug will rip that tiny top from her body, and I can feast on those beautiful tits. *Fuck*.

"Cal, I have done this before." I cut a glance to Ki as she pulls me from my dirty thoughts. Her incredulous stare makes me chuckle. All I offer is a smirk. It's the same procedure every time we tour. It's who I am. After all these years, I am the perfectionist. My mom taught me to be meticulous about details in my life. There is one detail I want to inspect with meticulous care — little Miss Quinn. I need to get out of here.

"I know. If you need me, I'm heading to the music room. Don't disturb me unless it's urgent. Tayla, good to see you wearing our merch." Her smile lights the room.

"Thank you. I love the tank." Once I have my coffee, I make my way to the staircase. In the music room, I close the door. As soon as I slip into the chair, my eyes shut. Visions of her scorch into my mind in so many positions until she's screaming my name.

TAYLA

Glancing at my phone, I see it's three-thirty. I am almost home. Work kept me busy, but my thoughts were filled with blue eyes and tattooed arms. Callum wasn't around today, so I spent my day with Ryan and Liam. They're so much fun. It was as if I was part of the team. There wasn't any animosity or frustration. Both were impressed at how quickly I set up the drums and keyboards. Working with the crew will be easy since they've been with the band for years.

I was in a good mood when I left and began walking home. It's warm out, and I revel in the vitamin D since I'm indoors most of the time. Also, I needed to clear my mind and calm myself down. Tonight is my dinner with Callum. I need my sister, so I send a quick text to Emma. We have missed each other online, and today I have to talk to her. My news will shock her. She knows how I felt, or feel rather, about Callum.

T: I am almost home. Skype in ten minutes?

I hit send. Fishing my keys from my purse, I unlock the door and step inside the quiet apartment. In the kitchen, I turn the kettle on and get my coffee cup ready. My mind is in a state of uncertainty at the prospect of spending the night with him. Alone. Back in the living room, I plug in my laptop to charge.

I wonder what I should wear? I cannot believe I agreed to do this. Not standing up to his challenge was not an option though. He would try his utmost to frustrate me. My sister will kill me when she finds out I'm going to dinner with Callum. She has had the biggest crush on him for ages. With his dark, messy spikes and sky-blue eyes, she's bewitched. Every time he posts a selfie on Twitter or Instagram, she goes absolutely nuts.

The kettle boils, and I make myself a coffee. Getting comfortable at my desk, I open Skype and log in. I see Emma is online already and hit the call button. "Hello, love! I have to tell you what happened. You will not bloody believe it." Her voice is loud and shrill, and her accent is slightly British. With a giggle, I sit back and sip the hot liquid. She always makes me laugh. The overly passionate personality bubbles through with every word she says. Her excitement over every aspect of her life is amazing. My heart races when I think about telling her the situation I got myself into. At twenty-eight, I'm older by three years, and I think it shows more often than not.

"What happened, Em?" She gushes about the guy she works with. Apparently, he is taking her to Paris Fashion Week. He's hot, rich, and well connected. I giggle at her enthusiasm. After twenty minutes of details, ranging from his favorite foods to the way his abs look when he's working out, I have a perfect idea of the man my sister is now head over heels for.

"So, what's your news? How is LA? And the new job?" She shoots questions at me, and when she eventually gives me a second to reply, I take a deep breath.

"LA hasn't changed since you left. My job . . . It's . . . Well, it's different. I mean, it's what I want to do, but it's scary." I keep quiet, hoping to buy time, but she presses me for more information.

"Yes, okay, who is the band? You said they're famous."

"Um . . . Well, I . . ." My phone beeps as I'm about to come clean.

"Tay, come on. Tell me? I can hear there's something you're not telling me."

I glance at the screen. There's a text from Callum.

C: Be ready at 7, and wear something . . . Stunning. I know you will.

My heart races again. I'm sure stunning wasn't what he wanted to say. Looking back up at the laptop monitor, I'm thankful we didn't do a video chat. "I'm going to dinner tonight with my boss, to, uhm . . . To welcome me." I cringe at the lie. "I mean, you know, to chat and stuff."

"Fucking hell, Tay, who is your boss? Do I have to drag it out of you?"

I grin. "It's Callum Hayes." Shutting my eyes, I wait for it, but she's silent. "Emma?" I'm met with stony silence. Finally, she clears her throat.

"Sorry, I think my speaker crackled. It sounded like you said you're going on a date with Callum? *The* Callum fucking Hayes! The one you don't like? You said he is an overconfident, self-absorbed asshole?" I realized this was coming.

"It's not a date; it is dinner. Nothing more. Emma, he is my boss. I'm part of the crew for their upcoming tour. It's a professional dinner." I'm not sure if I'm trying to convince myself or her. With hope it will calm her down, I stay silent.

"Fine, *but* if I see any tabloid pics of you kissing him, you're dead. I want the news first before anyone else. And if you're dating him, can you hook me up with his brother?" Finally, I hear her laugh, and the nervous tension that tightened my shoulders abates.

"Why on earth would I kiss Callum? And no, I will not hook you up with Liam. He's an asshole." The thought of kissing Callum runs through my mind, and the knot in my stomach tightens. He wouldn't try anything stupid. At least, I hope he won't. Emma's voice breaks through my thoughts.

"Don't be a dunce because he's Callum fucking Hayes! You will fall for him, love. I can guarantee that now. And we're sisters. It's important you hook me up, babe. I mean, Liam can bang my drums any day." I chuckle at her. Shaking my head, I realize she can't see me.

"You're terrible, Em. And I will not fall for Callum!"

Famous last words.

After my call with Emma, I get ready. She gave me an idea of what to wear, although her first option was way too sexy. I prefer a less revealing top to the one she suggested. A demure black silk cowl neck is what I settled on. The grey pants are straight cut, hugging my thighs and ass like a glove. I can tease him, even if we're not dating. My black, high-heeled boots will put me at roughly the same height as Callum. The outfit is stylish but relaxed. With my long, blonde hair pinned into a messy bun, I kept my makeup minimal. Since this isn't a date, I want to look as casual as possible. There are still fifteen minutes before Callum is picking me up. It was a good decision to get ready earlier, so I didn't rush around at the last minute.

The top covers my back; I made sure my tattoo wasn't visible. Tonight isn't the night I want to explain why my back is covered in ink. All Callum's girlfriends were inked, and I wonder if that was a conscious decision on his part. *Did he prefer girls with tattoos?*

The doorbell pulls me from my thoughts, and my stomach is in knots. *Calm down, Tay, it's a dinner.* Relax — deep breaths. As soon as I stand, my knees are wobbly. *Shit!* Annoyance at myself for allowing him to affect me heats my cheeks. He's just Callum. This is ridiculous. I need to get a grip. Walking over to the door, I twist the handle and when he comes into view, my breathing hitches. *Shit!* My eyes hungrily drink in the man in front of me. There is no doubt he actually put in some effort. He's wearing a black dress shirt, the first three buttons loose, hinting at the soft, smooth skin beneath. I can see glimpses of the tattoos covering his exquisite body. The sleeves are rolled up to his elbows, and the ink adorning his toned forearms looks incredible in the dim light of the hallway. My gaze slowly drops to his legs. The snug, dark blue jeans hug his thighs like they're molded to the muscle beneath. This will be harder than I thought. I have to admit; he looks incredible. "Callum." My voice comes out breathy, and I instantly regret it.

"How are you, Petal?" His eyes roam over the exposed skin of my shoulder. The heat of his intense gaze brands me, and an ache that is almost debilitating pulses between my thighs. A blush heats my cheeks instantly. This man will be the death of me.

"Come in." Stepping aside, I watch him walk into my apartment. He looks out of place in the living room. The door shuts with a click, and I turn to face him. The smirk on his lips unnerves me.

"I'm fine, Callum, thank you. So, it's Petal now?" I'm in for a challenge tonight. I can't stop staring at him, stunned by his ethereal beauty. His dark brown, spikey hair points in all directions, his ice-blue gaze is shimmering like diamonds in the low light.

"Yes. Your tattoo. It's beautiful. Soft and feminine. Like you. Mostly." His gaze rakes over the blossoms on my shoulder. Thankfully, my top covers the one on my back. I don't want or need him seeing that one.

"Mostly?" I question. Amusement is clear in his features.

"You come across as a hard-ass sometimes." His gaze travels from my face to my neck and over my breasts. It's such a slow movement it has my core clenching with suppressed desire. When he reaches my shoes, I recognize the dark glint in his eyes as his stare locks back on mine. "You scrub up well, Petal."

"Thank you, Callum. You can call me Tay."

Ignoring my statement, he smirks. "Are you ready, gorgeous?"

"Yes. Let's get this over with." Grabbing my purse, I shut my laptop and turn to him.

"You're not paying, so I suggest you leave that behind." He points at the purse in my hand.

"This isn't a date. I can pay for my dinner." With narrowed eyes, he shrugs and turns towards the door. After we step out, I turn and lock the apartment. Taking another deep breath, I spin on my heel and bump into his solid back. The scent of his cologne envelopes me, and goosebumps rise over my body.

"If you want to touch me, you could just ask." He narrows his gaze at me, and playfully grins before he strides down the hall, and walks down the staircase. I want to scream he infuriates me so much.

"Don't flatter yourself. You forget I am your intern," I retort, following him to the foyer.

As soon as we reach the entrance, he turns to face me, and his expression changes. I see a flicker of indignation. "You should lighten up, beautiful. Just enjoy yourself tonight."

I glance up into sky-blue eyes and smile. "Fine, I will lighten up when you realize this is *not* a date." We're face to face. Only inches apart, and his warm breath is on my face. He is handsome, with a rugged jaw. He hasn't shaved, and the five o'clock shadow looks enticing. His skin is smooth, not a wrinkle in sight. His lips are full and look so goddamn kissable. My teeth tug on my lower lip to keep from leaning up to plant my lips firmly on his. There's no doubt he is perfect. My tension eases before realizing who I am with. His cologne invades my senses again, and I can't tear my gaze away.

He grabs my hand. "Fine, it's a friendly dinner, but I guarantee that by the end of the night, you will agree to a second date." We make our way to the black Jeep parked in front of my building. He opens the door, and I slide into the passenger seat. I watch him walk around to the driver's side, moving with such grace and confidence. It's sexy, and I realize I'm blatantly staring. Once he slips into the seat, the engine purrs to life. The radio starts up, and I recognize his voice as Hunters in Oblivion's new song fills the car. "What's your favorite song on the latest album?" he asks, his eyes never leaving the road.

"'Damaged Angel,' no question about it."

He glances at me and smiles. "Really? Why?"

I open my mouth, then shut it again. There is no way I can tell him it saved my life. It's too personal. I've only just met him. "Uh, I love the lyrics. They speak to people on a personal level. Like you're talking directly to us. It's a beautiful song." I opt for a half-truth and hope he doesn't ask me any more questions. He gives a small nod and doesn't say another word. I watch the city lights pass as we make our way into town.

Ten minutes later, he pulls into a parking lot for a restaurant called Crossroads. Since it's a vegetarian restaurant, I'm looking forward to seeing what they have on the menu. I didn't have an inkling to eat vegetarian meals when I was studying. At that point, anything we could afford would do, mainly pizza. It seems Callum will be with me the first time I experience this. The warm feeling in my belly calms me. When his hand reaches for mine, I flinch, not expecting the spark to rush through my arm.

"Well, here we are. I hope you're feeling adventurous." He glances at me and smiles. He looks so excited, and I find the excitement bubbling inside me. It's the only non-date I have had in a while, and I want to enjoy it. He gets out and makes his way around the car. I take a deep breath, steadying my pulse to a regular pace. When he opens my door, I give him a genuine smile.

"Thank you, Callum." His fingers on my lower back send tingles down my spine as we make our way to the restaurant. His touch is so light I think I imagine it. But I'm too aware of the electric current radiating through my body at his fingertips heating my skin below the flimsy material of my top. The manager greets him and shows us to our table.

"Enjoy your evening, Mr. Hayes."

He walks off, leaving us alone. Callum pulls out my chair, and as I sit, I remark, "This place is fancy, Callum." He gives me a sweet smile, and I realized the naughty smirk is gone. That makes me more nervous. I prefer the annoying, arrogant Callum to the sweet one I have in front of me right now. Because I know the sweet one will weave his way under my skin and into my heart. I can now see why girls fall over themselves for him. Even though I can't be falling for him, I agree with my sister and every other female in the world — he is incredible.

"Only the best for my new intern." The

waiter arrives, and I'm grateful for the distraction. Callum orders a bottle of wine and a starter for us to share while we settle on dinner. Picking up my menu, my eyes drop to the prices, and I gasp. The prices of the dishes are exorbitant. I know Callum can afford it. The extravagance is something he's used to.

The waiter, back a couple minutes later with the wine, pours a taster, and Callum takes a sip, then nods to the waiter to fill our glasses. The waiter leaves the bottle on the table and retreats. Once again, we're alone. "I would like to propose a toast." He lifts his drink, and I follow his lead. "To changing your preference." He clinks my glass.

"In your dreams, Hayes," I add with a giggle and take a sip of my wine. He stares into my eyes and winks, the gesture sending a tremble over my body. The menu is filled with dishes I have only ever heard of. Everything sounds good, but I have no idea what tastes good. Moments later, the waiter brings our starter. The service is impeccable, and I wonder if it's because he's Callum Hayes, or because they're just that good. Glancing down at the platter, I realize there's enough food to feed a small army. Everything looks incredible, and the smells are enticing. My mouth waters and I realize I skipped lunch. Work kept me busy.

"Are you ready to order?" The waiter's gaze falls to me, then to Callum.

Cerulean eyes settle on me. "Do you trust

me?" Those words and his gaze snag me in a sudden rush of tingles. I nod. He glances at the waiter and places the order for our main course. Once the waiter disappears, Callum turns to me again.

"I hope you can relax tonight. Enjoy this. I realize you're not like the other women, Tayla. And the tabloids paint an awful picture of me. However, they don't know the real me." I take in his expression.

"So, your persona they depict of you isn't true? You don't go out partying and picking up girls whenever you want to?" His stare pierces me, and I instantly feel lousy for what I said.

"Yes, I have a colorful past. I have done those things you've read. Not now. I can prove it to you, but first, tell me why you're so serious? You're very uptight. I need to know you, Tay. You intrigue me. I like to be intrigued." The smirk that curls his full lips has me blushing — still my annoyance bristles.

"I guard myself against getting hurt. My past has made me wary. Someone hurt me. So, I don't talk about it. Other than that, I'm an open book." His eyes sear into me as if he can see inside me. The arctic blue of his eyes sparkles in the dim light of the restaurant.

"Tell me what made you study sound engineering." I take another sip of wine.

"The music industry has been a dream for me. I'm not a singer or performer. Being in front of millions of people isn't my thing. Not that I get stage fright, but it's just not me."

He nods and smiles. "That's understandable. It's not for everyone." His gaze drops to the table as he ponders on a thought. Looking back up, locking his eyes on mine, he asks, "Why do you push so much? I mean, I don't expect you to jump me." He chuckled at that. "But you're closed off. Very much so." He sounds genuinely curious. *How do I answer that?* I averted my gaze from his and try to gather my thoughts.

"My trust in men has been tarnished. I was hurt before in a way that doesn't allow me to open up easily." He stares at me as if trying to find another answer inside my mind.

"So, if I was persistent and proved you can trust me . . . I mean, if you could trust me, would you be so inclined?" Those heated blue pools darken to a beautiful midnight blue. Deep, captivating, and frightening as fuck. He knows his intense scrutiny unnerves me. The effect he has on women isn't lost on him; it's clear. I pick up my glass. Stalling. Thinking.

"No." His chuckle at my response rumbles in his chest, giving me a perfect smile that makes panties melt the world over. Here I am, sitting across from him, and I can't fathom why he chose me.

"I like you, Tayla. No situation is too challenging for me, and you're no exception." I peer at him in awe at his blatant honesty. My mouth falls open and words evade me. I swallow thickly. Emotion washes over me in waves.

"Honestly, I'm difficult to win over. I'm not the woman for you. Also, you seem sure of yourself, Callum. We are working together. Or, at least, I work for you. You realize this is dangerous territory?" He nods calmly, assessing my answer. We stare at each other. It's silent for so long. I think we'll spend the rest of the night just sitting in silence.

"Petal, let me tell you something. I have a past. Some things make it difficult for me to trust women. Why do you think I'm single? And have been for a long time." There were rumors about him and his ex-girlfriend. Apparently, she used him. The details aren't clear, but the hatred for her by fans is unmistakable. Something happened; I want to know what.

"This shouldn't impact my job. I don't want to be known for sleeping with my boss to get where I am." My words are final. He nods.

"It won't. I promise. I know you think you can't trust me, but I will prove to you that you can. Besides, I want to take you somewhere tonight," he blurts, and his eyes search mine. "To show you my favorite place in the world." His smile is beautiful. It lights up his clear blue eyes. "Trust me? Even if only for tonight?" I don't have to think about my answer as the impulse to trust nags at me. I can trust him. It's the look in his eyes that scares me, holding me hostage.

"Yes, Callum, I can."

He smiles. "Good, that's my girl!" I'm drawn in by the man I'm fighting my attraction to. This isn't good. Not good at all.

The rest of dinner was relaxed. He didn't ask me anything personal. We chatted about being on tour. It sounds like we'll tour Europe first and then heading back to the States before heading off to the Southern Hemisphere. As we drive through the quiet streets, I realize we're headed up to the Griffith Observatory.

It's been a while since I was here. My time at college brought us up here most nights when we would bring a bottle of Jack, get drunk, and look at the stars and the twinkling city lights. With sneaky glances at Callum, my stomach flutters when the streetlights pass and illuminate his profile. The angular jaw dusted with stubble. The need to run my fingers over his face is intense.

Uncertainty crawls in my mind. Why he wants *me*. He could have his pick of models, actresses, or any other woman. I mean, he's Callum fucking Hayes. As terrified as I am at my feelings for this man, I promised him I would enjoy the night. That's what I intend to do. When I open my eyes, I notice him glancing at me. "You okay, Petal?" His nickname for me makes me smile. I nod.

"Yes, it's been a long day." When he reaches over and places his hand on my thigh, my core tightens with a dull ache. A need I don't want. Or have even entertained in years. Too long. My skin tingles below the material of my pants at his touch, and my stomach flip-flops. It's been almost a year since I was with anyone. A man's touch, it's foreign to me. I'm still scared. The fear claws at me when I think about it. Of being naked with someone.

"I promise not to keep you out too late. There's something I want you to see." When he drives up toward the observatory, I grin. This is one of my favorite places in the city as well.

"I haven't been here since my third year in college." My words are heavy with emotion as the memories of being happy flood me.

"Come on. Let's go have a look." I open the car door, slipping out, and stand in awe. The stars are bright, the new moon a sliver in the dark sky. You can see the whole city below, lights as far as the eye can see. It really is a breathtaking view. I turn to him, "Callum, thank you. I forgot how beautiful it was up here." He takes my hand, and we walk toward the edge where we can get a better view.

"The city of damaged angels." A strong emotion races through me, and tears threaten. I blink hard to stop myself from crying. After the turmoil and heartache, I needed to escape my old life. Now, here I am in the very place I gave up because the pain was too much to handle. Here I stand holding the hand of a man I least expected to have standing next to me. It's overwhelming.

He cuts a glance to me. "Hey, now. No crying. I don't make women cry." The tears come like a waterfall now. Embarrassment floods me. Here I am crying in front of one of the most famous men in the world. He turns me toward him and swipes my wet cheeks with the pads of his thumbs. His touch soft, smooth, and my eyes flutter closed, reveling in the sensation. His soft lips are on mine suddenly, and I jumped back. "Callum! What are you doing?" He looks sheepish and gone is the arrogant man.

"Sorry. I didn't mean to. I got caught up in the moment, and you looked so beautiful. I wanted to kiss away your tears." He glances down and turns away, facing the city again. His walls come up, and his expression is suddenly guarded. He let it down in that instant, and somehow, I let mine down too. In the dim light that surrounded us, I saw a broken man surface.

"Callum . . ." He shakes his head.

"It's okay, Tay. I understand. Maybe you do like my brother. It's always him. No matter how badly he treats girls, they always flock to him."

His words puzzle me. "No, I don't like Liam. But what are you talking about? There are multitudes of girls who would kill to be with you." He chuckles, and his gaze meets mine.

"Yes. I suppose there are, but none of them grab my attention . . ." He turns, his body facing me entirely. The smile on his face is gentle. "Only you." My breath catches in my throat. *What? What did he mean?* I'm an average woman, nothing special. *Wait, no, this is his sweet talking! Isn't it?* He confuses and infuriates me, but this sensitive part is weaving its way into my heart.

"What? I caught your attention by spilling coffee over you?" He laughs and nods.

"I guess so, yes. You're challenging and confident and so fucking stubborn. I admire that in a woman. Someone who can give me a run for my money." His words sink in. Thoughts are whirling through my mind. Never have I been complimented by a man like him. I stare at the stars above us. They twinkle with a promise. If I can learn to trust him, this could work. *Do I want it to?*

"I speak my mind, Callum, and I am stubborn because you infuriate me more than you know." When I walk toward him, I hold out my hand. "I love challenging you. It's fun. This" — I point between us — "it's new to me. You have to understand that a relationship is difficult for me." He laces his fingers through mine. "Let's not talk now. How about you drive me home?" I smile and tug him toward the car.

We ride in comfortable silence to my apartment. He pulls up to the sidewalk, and I realize I don't want the night to end just yet. He speaks first. "I hope you enjoyed the dinner and the city lights." I can hear the smile in his voice but don't face him. I wouldn't get out of his car if I saw those blue pools that pierce my soul. Thoughts of kissing him are at the forefront of my mind now. "Petal?"

Against my better judgment and against every ounce of restraint I have, I turn to him and whisper, "Did you want to come up? For a drink?" A smile that threatens to crack his face appears, and he nods.

"I would."

I turn on the lights as we enter the living room. Inside my tiny space again, his scent invades the room. "Make yourself comfortable. I'm just going to change."

"Into something slinky and sexy, I hope?" My glare quietens his chuckle immediately. "I was kidding. You need to lighten up, Petal." His words say one thing, but the hungry gaze traveling over my body says something different.

Once in the safety of my bedroom, I change into a tank top and a pair of sweats. Fully aware of Callum sitting in my living room, my body is tingling in anticipation. This will be interesting. There is nothing that can prepare you for Callum Hayes on your sofa. Relaxed. Sexy. Perfect. He has taken his jacket off, and the shirt he wore hugs every muscle in his torso and chest. "Tea, coffee, wine, beer, or water?" I grin. His eyes sparkle, taking in my casual appearance. The heat of his stare warms my skin, and the knot in my belly tightens. I'm in so much trouble.

"Wow, what a selection. Wine will be a perfect start."

"Start? Are you planning on staying that long?" I giggle. *Since when do I giggle? Seriously.*

He winks, and that cocky arrogance is back. "As long as you want me." I shake my head as I stride toward the kitchen. Grabbing two wine glasses out of the cupboard, I place them on the counter and select a red wine. Not that my collection is that big. Once the bottle is open, I half-fill both glasses.

I feel him before I turn. His body radiating heat toward me. He has won this round because I'm helplessly aching to be near him. To have his body against mine. When I turn — slowly — I'm careful not to spill wine over him. I peer up through my eyelashes, and those intense, deep-blue eyes are staring down at me. His tongue flicks out, moistening his soft pink lips, and the gesture sends a tingle straight to my clit. My pussy pulses with need.

"Thank you." He takes the glass from my hand. When his fingers brush against mine, I almost drop the glass. The way he holds my gaze has my panties melting. My need for him surpasses every rational thought in my head. I need to put distance between us. He's too close. Desire swirls thick in the surrounding air.

"Callum." I breathe his name. My voice is low, raspy, and I chide myself for letting him get to me this much. Even though his name is a warning on my lips, he ignores it and leans down. Instinctively, my eyes flutter closed. His lips feather mine, and this time, I have nowhere to go. He reaches behind me and sets his glass down on the counter. He frees me of my glass and grips my hips in a vice-like hold, pulling me into him — his rock-hard body flush against mine. Every ridge and plane of those sculpted abs press against me. I'm lost, just for the moment. I let myself go in that minute. I give in and let this annoying man kiss me. *I am so fucked.*

I run my fingers through his soft hair and completely forget about anything around me. He growls into my mouth as his tongue twirls with mine. It's such a sensual dance that my panties are soaked with arousal. I'm fully aware of his erection pressing against my stomach. I have to catch my breath. He needs to stop, and I need to stop. My control slipped, but I have to get it back. This situation overwhelms me. I place my hands on his chest, and I can feel his muscles tense. A low groan vibrates under my touch.

The taste of him is intoxicating. With a slow push, he reluctantly breaks the kiss. He holds my face in his hands and looks deep into my eyes as the pad of his thumb brushes over my lower lip. His voice is hoarse. Filled with desire as he whispers, "Now that is a first kiss." Reaching behind me, he picks up his wine glass. Turning, he walks into the living room, leaving me reeling from the most amazing kiss I've ever had. I pick up my wine, gulping a mouthful, then refill my glass. As I walk back into the living room, he smiles like nothing happened.

"Well, that was . . ." My words trail off, and I can't find an apt description. Callum pats the space beside him on the sofa, and I sit down, watching him.

"Yes, that was," he replies in his low timbre. It seems we're both stunned. I definitely wasn't expecting a kiss with Callum Hayes to be so good. Well, that's a lie, I knew it would be. A small smile spreads across my face, and he notices. "Did I bring on that smile?" he inquires, I nod slowly.

"You surprised me, nothing more." He reaches out, starting at my shoulder, tracing a slow feather-light path down my arm. It sends electric currents shooting over my skin. Goosebumps rose in the wake of his touch and I shiver involuntarily.

"You do realize that you're beautiful," he whispers.

"Callum, I'm just an average girl. Please don't say things like that?" He sits forward, his fierce gaze burning into me.

Ignoring my request, he murmurs, "You couldn't be more wrong. Average doesn't even begin to describe what you are, Tayla Quinn."

He sets his glass down on the coffee table and leans in toward me. My body reacts to his proximity and my lips tingle. My mind pleads for him to kiss me again. And when his lips meet mine, my eyes flutter closed and the stars behind my eyelids sparkle. The heat of his kiss travels over my feverish skin, and my pussy pulses with need. My clit throbs for his fingers to tease me; to slide into me. My panties nearly disintegrate when his hand grips my thigh, then continues to tease its way higher. His kiss scorches me. His touch ignites my skin. A primal growl from low in his throat tightens the desire in my belly. Slowly, he moves over me. Our bodies in sync as I lie back, welcoming him as he nudges between my thighs. Our tongues glide sensually over each other in a seductive dance. With his body hovering over me, his one hand slips down and grips my hip. My molten core is a volcano waiting to erupt. The scorching lava flows through my veins.

My top has ridden up, and his fingers finally come into contact with my skin. A low mewl escapes my lips, and he swallows it in the kiss. With a leisurely caress, his fingertips find a path to the underwire of my bra. He knows how to touch. Soft. Light. Making me moan into his mouth. My body arches up toward him. He licks into me, tasting me — and the wine — as I taste him. I'm drunk. Although wine has nothing to do with the heady feeling, he's claiming me with just this one kiss.

"Callum." His name comes out softer than I mean. Breathy. Raspy. He knows I want him, and if I don't stop this now, we will do something we shouldn't be doing. The moment is broken, and the magic that spiraled around us dissipates, and our eyes lock for the longest time.

"Petal, I'm sorry. I couldn't help myself. I haven't been so attracted to someone in a long time." He moves off me, and I sit up slowly, immediately missing the heat of his body. Every inch of my skin tingles, and I notice his rock-hard length straining against his slacks.

"Look, Callum, I'm sorry. It's just . . ."

He places his hand on my knee, and another shockwave travels through me. When he peers up, my heartaches. He looks sad. If he only realized I've never been this attracted to anyone my whole life. With just a kiss, a small touch, my body comes alive.

"It's okay. I understand." I put my hand over his.

"No, you don't. I can't do this. Romantic relationships with someone you work with can add extra pressure. More tension."

"That doesn't bother me, Petal. Unless you have someone?" I glance at him, a frown creasing my eyebrows. *Someone?* When the realization hits me, I want to giggle.

"God, no! I haven't had someone in years. I mean . . . I mean not . . . Uhm . . . Shit. I mean, I'm not seeing someone." Abruptly, I stand. His stare is too much, too intense. My heart races, and I'm not sure what I want to say. "People will talk, and I can't afford to lose my job. You're a rock star. What will people think? Your friends and family?" He gets up, the irritation visible in his features and his stance. He grabs my shoulders and spins me around. When he pulls me toward him, I stop breathing. Our bodies are once again remarkably close, and I can't think straight.

"Tayla, stop. Just for one second, stop and don't worry about what everyone else will assume. Stop worrying about the rules. What the fuck do you want? Open yourself up and stop being so fucking stubborn." Sky-blue eyes turn stormy, and it takes him shouting at me to realize I want him to kiss me. Without another word, his mouth crashes down on mine, and I don't care. I don't stop him. Kissing him back, I'm surprised by how much I want it. How much I want him.

The past I worked so hard to keep buried better stay buried. Because if I'm going to do this with him, he can't know what happened.

Glancing down, the lights shining on me hide the eyes that are glued to me. I swirl around the soft fabric holding me up in the air. Their hungry gazes are locked on my every move. They anticipate my movements, holding their breath. From this high up, they can't see the girl beneath the façade I portray. The scars that have marred my skin. It's okay. I did it to keep my sister safe. There isn't a day that goes by I regret what I did. But she was safe. This was my final performance. He made sure of it, and his promise will be kept, but there is no choice for me. I had to leave. The burn on my skin still aches from last night.

I am upside down. He's here. I can feel his filthy leer on me. I need to finish my routine. My heart shudders in my chest. He came back. After all he did. I can't hide. That's what he told me. Fear grips me, and I almost fall. I take a deep breath and swirl down in a slow, effortless movement. The song slows to a stop, and the applause deafens me. He's watching. Waiting. I offer the crowd a small smile. Walking off the stage, I make my way to my dressing room. The girls up next pass me on the way, and then I am alone with my thoughts. Alone. He will follow me. I wait for it.

CALLUM

As soon as I walked into the house last night, or should I say early this morning, I realized I would get the third degree today. Liam knew I had taken Tayla out, but what he didn't know was she wants me. That much is obvious. Even though we didn't fuck, her body told me all I need to know. Nothing will stop me from ripping her panties off or sliding them down her legs. As I roll over in bed, I glance at the clock. Fuck, it's only eight on a Friday morning. There's so much shit to do. I'm not in the frame of mind.

Last night differed from past dates. We just sat on her sofa, chatting, drinking wine, and learning more about each other as the night turned to morning. I didn't get home until five a.m. There would be no stopping both Liam and Kierra from asking me shit loads of questions I don't want to answer.

Ki is worried about me getting involved with someone who works with us. Liam will ask how tight she is. My brother can be crude. He loves women, lots of them. Sometimes at the same time. But for me, only one woman outshines the rest.

The memory of Tayla's lips on mine is seared into my mind. Her body so pliable against mine, under my touch. In my control. That beautiful blonde hair fanned over her pillows when I left her, haunts me. It took all my self-control to walk out. We had taken things slow. She told me she's not ready to get into a serious relationship.

Though I highly doubt it will be long before she is waking up next to me. Naked. I can't wait to see what her sweet little body looks like without the barrier of material. That ass is perfect, fitting into my hand. Glancing down at the tent in my sheets, I grip my hard shaft. I stroke it with thoughts of her running through my mind. Her soft lips would feel so good wrapped around me. I want to fuck her sassy little mouth with those beautiful eyes staring up at me.

My fist moves faster over my hard cock, imagining her sucking me deep into her throat, fucking all that sass and cheekiness away. Then taking her body and bending her over my piano. Watching that pert little ass as I ram into her. Deeper. Harder. Until she's crying out my fucking name. Callum fucking Hayes. My body tenses, and my release shoots over my stomach. As soon as I open my eyes, I take a deep breath. I want this woman, and nothing will stop me from having her.

Grabbing my shirt from the empty side of the sheets, I clean myself up and hop out of bed.

A shower, then I need to work. This fucking melody in my head needs of an outlet. The warm spray is calming. Thoughts of Tay invade my mind again. I have to figure out a way of getting her to trust me. After talking to her last night, I realize she's different from the groupies we typically have hanging around. She's intelligent, mysterious, sexy, and I need her. I knew one night with me would get her over her apprehension about being with me because we work together. She will be mine. All fucking mine. Once I'm out of the shower, I wrap a towel around my waist.

"Callum!" Liam's voice is shrill from my bedroom. As I enter, I find him standing there looking like someone stole his coffee. *What the hell is wrong now?*

"What the fuck is your problem?"

"The label called. We have to have three songs ready by Friday next week. We have eight days."

"Fine. Done. What else?" His incredulous stare is piercing through me. Questions dance in his eyes and I wait for it. My brother doesn't disappoint.

"So, I guess the date went well?" The smirk curls his lips, and I hate that he knows me so well. He assumes I had sex with her. *Well, surprise brother, I didn't.*

"It was good. We didn't fuck. If that's what you're thinking? And she's not that type of girl." His laugh echoes through my room. I pull out a new T-shirt from my closet and tug it over my head.

"Not that type of girl? Are you going soft on me, brother?"

My glare cuts to him. "No, I don't want to fuck up with our intern. Tayla isn't a fucking groupie. She does work with us, after all."

"So, you're being a gentleman?" He flops onto my bed as I walk out of my closet dressed in my ripped black jeans with my "$uck It" tee. "Bro, be careful. We don't know if we can trust her. What if she sells the story after she's done with her contract?"

"That won't happen. Jesus, what the fuck is wrong with you?" My heart lurches at the thought of her being like the other groupies we have. She's not. My feelings for her shouldn't be so protective, and my brother knows it. He can see it in my expression.

"I'm just saying, man. You don't even know her."

"Neither do you. Get off my back about this, brother." He gets up and turns toward the door. I watch him shrug and walk out, shutting it behind him. I can't believe Liam is always such a dick, yet the girls flock to him. I need to stop thinking about this. My phone buzzing on the nightstand grabs my attention. Unlocking the screen, I find a message from Tay.

T: *Good morning, boss. I will be a few minutes late. The queue at the coffee shop is insane.*

C: Okay, Petal. We have a busy day, and my brother is driving me fucking insane.

T: Would you like me to spill coffee over him? I'm pretty good at that! LOL

I chuckle at her making fun of herself. She's adorable. Liam is right, I don't know her, but my gut tells me I'm right. There is no way she would do something like selling a goddamn story to the press.

C: I don't want you doing that. He may just want to take you out. That's not a good idea.

T: Why?

C: I want to keep you to myself. I don't like sharing. My brother, on the other hand, he does.

Slipping my phone in the pocket of my jeans, I make my way into the kitchen. I want coffee and then I need to get this song finished. "Cal, dude." I turn to find Ryan leaning against the doorjamb.

"What's up, man?"

"Your brother stormed out of here. What's going on with you two?"

"Nothing. He's being a dick, and I called him out on it. I'm not in the mood for his shit. It's fucking annoying. He needs to pull his head out of his ass. This whole bad-boy, fuck-up game he's playing is getting old."

"I know, but we need him right now. The more you fight, the more you push him away."

With a shrug, I grab my mug and walk toward the door. Ryan looks tired. We all are. The record label wants this album out as soon as possible. I'm a perfectionist with my music; I'm not submitting something that's not perfect. "I know. I can't deal with it now. I heard we need three songs ready, and there's a lot to get through today. Plus, I'm writing today. Do you need me down here?"

"No. I'm working on the keyboard for the last track we did. I'll be in the studio with Tayla."

At the mention of her name, my heart lurches. "Call me if there are any issues." I turn and make my way upstairs into the music room — my sweet little piece of heaven. Setting my phone and coffee down, I slip into the seat. I inhale a deep breath, position my hands over the ivory keys. As my fingers dance over the black and white pads, bringing the melody to life, I grin. It's been in my head for the past week. I close my eyes. Blonde hair and brown eyes flit through my mind.

My fingers fly over the keys gently. The tune is beautiful; I need to write it down, but I can't stop. Not right now. The echoes of the keyboards and guitars downstairs filter up through the air vent, and I feel the song with every beat of my heart. My pulse races and the notes possess me. I am not stopping until I reach that last chord.

And before I'm ready for it to end, it's

finished. The song in my head brought to life. "Fuck." My voice is a rough growl. I've never had something hit me so deeply. To my very soul. Grabbing a notepad and pen, I jot down every note — every key. The melody on paper doesn't look right, but when you hear it . . . Something about it courses through my veins. I don't have a title, and it's far from complete, but something tells me this will hit number one.

The buzzing of my phone pulls me from my thoughts. I pick it up to see Tayla's name flash on the screen. I hit the green button. "Hello, Petal."

"Callum, I wish you wouldn't call me that."

"Why? You're gorgeous, delicate, and sweet, well . . . That I still need to find out."

Her musical, soft laugh makes me smile. I envision her beautiful brown eyes sparkling with amusement at my silliness. "Cal, don't be ridiculous. Just letting you know I'm downstairs. Ryan said you were writing. I didn't want to disturb the genius at work."

"That's okay, Petal. Any disruption from you is welcome."

"I have to get back to work." Her voice is low and so goddamn adorable.

"Have fun, Petal. I need to get a song written. I'm under pressure to finish three songs by Friday." Her gasp across the line sends a jolt of heat to my crotch, and I'm suddenly rock hard.

"Will you be able to do it?"

"I think so. I will see you in a bit, okay?"

"Okay." I can hear the grin in her voice. I

hang up. A knock on the door startles me. When I twist to find Ki, I realize I'm in for my second round of third degree.

"You hiding?"

"Writing." Her eyes narrow, and I know what she's thinking. Kierra is a shrewd pain in my ass, but I can't do anything without her noticing. I wait for the question burning in her stare.

"Is it Tayla inspiring you?"

"Why?" My voice comes across harsher than I want it to, and she smirks. Kierra did it on purpose, and She knows me too well. This will not blow up in my face.

"I know it is, Callum. You're an open book. Let me warn you . . ." She strides into the room until she's close enough to slap me. She doesn't. Instead, she prods me in the chest. "If you fuck this up, I will fuck you up. *Do. Not. Break. Her. Heart.*" With every word another stab.

"Kierra, I am not planning on breaking her heart. Just relax." I notice Ryan watching us from the doorway. I knew he had a crush on Kierra. The problem is, he doesn't have the balls to ask her out. Granted, she's difficult. Since her ex left her because she took her job so seriously, she's steered clear of men.

Most people think I'm dating her, which is a fucking joke. I wouldn't and could never date Kierra. She's only three years my junior, but I see her as a younger sister. Ryan is a good guy. I hope he gets his head out of his ass before someone else moves in on her. She won't be there forever.

"Ki, we need you in the office." She turns and walks out, leaving me chuckling. The door nudges again. This time, my beautiful girl is standing there.

"May I come in?"

"Absolutely, Ms. Quinn." I wink, which earns me a blush.

"How is the song coming?"

"It's perfect. I finally got the melody, which is the most challenging. I will write the lyrics later. Can I take you to lunch?"

She shakes her head. "You can't. I have work in the studio. A quick snack has to suffice. I'm helping Ryan with the sound for the track he laid down yesterday."

"Okay. I should join you downstairs and keep you company." She nods and leaves me to finish my writing. It's Friday, and I can't work over the weekend. I have plans for my sweet Petal. Hopefully, it proves I'm sincere.

TAYLA

I roll over, trying to find the horrendous noise waking me on a Saturday morning. My heavy eyelids open gradually, and I grab my phone. I notice the time and can't help groaning. It's not my alarm, but a text from Callum. I open the message. A loud gasp escapes my lips. "Fuck."

C: Be ready in an hour, I want to take you somewhere. C. xo

Shit, shit, shit! I scrambled out of bed and raced to the kitchen, turning on the kettle. Running back to the bedroom, I grab my towel from the rack. I looked terrible. Callum and I spent the evening talking — about music, movies, friends, traveling. Any subject we could think of. We only said goodbye at four a.m., and now I'm scrambling around my apartment getting ready for a surprise he has planned. There's something insatiable about the way he makes me feel. Every time we're together, it's as if we've known each other our whole lives. The only thing I can't talk about is the one night that changed my attitude toward men. My body lacerated, my heart crushed. I broke, but I also got stronger.

I pull on a pair of jeans and a long-sleeved tee. That will keep me warm since the weather is chilly this early in the morning. I tug my hair into a messy bun. As soon as I step into the living room, the doorbell buzzes. I grip the door handle and take a deep breath before I open it, coming face to face with the handsome man I'm slowly falling for. He's dressed casually, but breathtaking as always.

Dark blue jeans hug his thighs, snagging my attention, and I can't help drinking in his appearance. The fitted grey Henley he's wearing molds to his torso and chest, a black leather jacket hanging open, and he has on a pair of black biker boots. His short hair stands in every direction. It looks like he's just gotten out of bed. My stomach flutters when he grins. "Callum." A mischievous glint sparkles in his eyes.

"Petal, how are you this morning?"

"Good, I think."

"You ready?" He leans forward and wraps his arms around me. The warmth of his body pressed against me has my nerves fluttering. Instinctively, my arms circle his taut waist. The sweet-spicy scent of his cologne calms me. A mix of cinnamon and sandalwood, reminding me of sitting in front of the fire on a chilly winter's night. I step back, and he follows me into the apartment.

"I was surprised by your message this morning. We agreed to see each other later."

"I got the surprise I have planned confirmed. It's cold outside. Grab a jacket. You'll freeze in that little scrap of material." The heat of his gaze roams over my tight-fitting tee, heating me to the core from the top of my head to my feet. Fire coils deep in my stomach, tightening the ball of need that's ever-present when he's near. My pulse riots against my ribcage.

"Okay, I'll be back. Take a seat." Turning to the bedroom, I open my closet and pull out my thick, black pullover and find a hoodie. Checking my reflection in the mirror, I notice the flush on my cheeks. My hair is pinned perfectly with wisps that frame my face. I kept my makeup light. In the living room, I grab my purse. "Ready." I spin around.

"You look incredible, Petal." A blush spreads across my face.

"Thank you, rock star. So where are we going?"

"I want to show you California. In a way you never seen it. I hope you'll like it. You're not scared of heights, are you?" That sounds intriguing.

"No, I'm not. As long as we're not jumping out of a plane, I should be fine." He helps me pull on my hoodie. "You're being sweet, Hayes." He chuckles quietly.

"I'm a sweet guy, regardless of what the tabloids say." I know he's baiting me.

"Oh? So, you aren't a bad-boy rock star?"

He shakes his head slowly, his eyes searching mine. "You know, sometimes the things you read are exaggerated. Yes, I have done foolish things. Times where I was the bad boy, but I'm not that person anymore. I am thirty-five years old, Tay. I'm not sure what I want in ten years, but I know what I want right now." He stands so close my body reacts. His soft, large hands cup my face, and I stare into the deep blue pools — a window to his soul. The only thing I can think about are his lips on mine. "Let's go, or we'll be late." The low rasp of his voice rumbles, prickling my skin. A small smile curls my lips, and I nod.

"Okay," I breathe. He shuts his eyes for a second as if savoring our proximity. His thumbs swipe a slow arch on my cheeks, leaving a fiery blaze in their wake. This is such a bad idea, on so many levels. I'm falling. Fast and hard. We're flying in three weeks, and I have no way of knowing if, once he steps onto the plane, he will forget about me. I need just to quit thinking about that. Enjoying time with him is what I should focus on. When we're on tour, if he wants to go back to his groupies, as much as it hurts, I have to deal with it.

We make our way outside, and I notice he has a motorbike. I gasp in shock. It's gorgeous. Black and gleaming with streaks of ice blue and silver. It's a Suzuki GSX-R750. An extraordinary piece of machinery. It's been years since I was first on one. Never on one with this amount of power. The adrenaline that comes with the rumble of horsepower between your legs is exciting.

"You like her?" His face is pure amusement.

"Her?" I giggle.

"Yes, she's one of the girls in my life." With heated stare and sexy smirk, he picks up the helmets. Pulling my hair out of the bun, I make a low ponytail. Before I can ask what he means, he helps me slip on the matte black helmet, shutting the visor. He swings a leg over the seat, then holds a hand out. I slip mine in his and climb on fluidly. Thank God for yoga. I don't want to embarrass myself.

Suddenly, I'm aware of the fact that he's between my thighs. My arms wrap around his taut torso. His body tenses as my hold tightens. "Hold on tight, Petal." He turns the key, and the bike roars to life. The vibration of the sportbike and Callum's body against mine has me squirming. My pussy pulses and my panties are already wet. When I'm with him, I go into sexual overdrive. He speeds off, and the power vibrates through me. We hit the highway, and when he opens up the engine, we're flying. The scenery whizzing past us.

As soon as we go through the first turn, I close my eyes, holding him close against me as we lean to the side, my body following his. I notice his toned abs stiffen under my touch, which is ridiculously sexy. The ocean is a blur, streaking blue and white as the waves crash onto the shore. I can't help smiling as I consider where I am. This is every girl's dream, and here I am. My history with men hasn't been pleasant. I can't remember when I was just content with someone. Enjoying the moment.

When Callum veers off the tar road, I glance around as we slow. We come to a stop outside an enormous warehouse, the gravel crunching below the tires, and he stops under a tree. He reaches back and holds out a hand to help me off the bike. I tug the helmet off and run my fingers through my hair. With a quick glance up at the signboard, I beam. Since I was young, I've wanted to do this. It's been on my bucket list. A hot-air balloon is romantic. He's pulling out all the stops. I stifle a giggle and can't stop my heart racing.

"We're doing that?" I point, my voice comes out louder than I expect. He grins and nods.

"Yes, I figured I would show you how beautiful California is. A view from up in the air." My body quivers with excitement. Leaning up on my tiptoes, I drape my arms around his neck and snuggle into his jacket. He encircles me in a firm grasp, holding me in such a powerful but gentle way. When I release him from my hold and step back, he smiles with sparkling eyes. His nose crinkles. It's the cutest thing I have ever seen. He's so rugged and handsome. I'm the luckiest girl in the world.

His hair is now a mess after he's taken his helmet off. I crave to run my fingers through it and tug him toward me. He laces his fingers with mine, and we stroll into the large building. Once we find the welcome desk, the older woman looks up, offering a pleasant smile. "Mr. Hayes, great to see you back. They're almost ready for you. Everything you requested is set up. Enjoy your flight."

"Thank you," he responds, as we pass to the rear of the warehouse. A large yellow, red, and blue hot-air balloon is being fired up.

"Mr. Hayes. Perfect timing. We're ready. Please follow me." The man strides toward the basket and opens the hatch. "Hello, little lady." He grins.

"Hi." We step inside, and he bolts it. As he loosens the ropes holding us down, my stomach flip-flops. My grip on the edge tightens as we gradually drift up. Callum stands behind me, his arms on either side of me, caging me in. For the first time in a long while, I feel safe.

"Don't be scared. I got you. I hope you enjoy this, Petal." His voice is low as he murmurs in my ear. The heat of his breath on my neck sends delicious shivers over my body. His solid frame flush against mine. That taut torso against my back. He didn't shave this morning, and the scruff on his face tickles my cheek, which has me imagining how it would feel between my thighs.

I squirm at the image in my mind and suppress a giggle. "I guess you have done it, completely surpassed yourself, rock star." His chuckle vibrates through his chest. He's so warm; even though we're high in the sky, I'm cold at all.

"Anything for you." His murmur causes another set of goosebumps to erupt over my sensitive skin. The molten lava swirling in my stomach has my core pulsing. We look around, with Callum pointing out the sights. From up here, the city is breathtaking.

"How many girls have you brought up here?" As soon as the question is out, I regret it. *Did I want to know?* No, I can't think about Cal with anyone else. That realization shocks me. We've only stolen a kiss here and there, so I didn't consider us serious. This past week he spent in the music room, and work has kept me busy, learning how to edit videos, setting up the instruments for both Ryan and Liam, and working with Kierra on most of the tour details. I had seen more of her than Callum.

"You really want to know?" I nod. I don't really want to know, but the sadist in me needs the torture. "None. I haven't dated girls before, Tayla. It's never been something I wanted or needed. This right here" — he gestures around us — "it's new to me too." I find myself relaxing back into his toned chest. With a small smile, I revel in the honesty he's just given me.

We were in the air for two hours, and Callum held onto me the whole trip. I was in awe of how beautiful it was. As we descended, a lightheaded feeling came over me. I hadn't eaten that morning because I was too tense to have anything other than coffee. As we approach the bike, he peers at me with a grin that melts my panties. "How about we grab lunch?"

"Yes, please. I'm starving. Since I was whisked away so early, I didn't have time to eat." When I glance up, his sky-blue eyes twinkle with amusement. "Thank you for today. It was unbelievable." He leans in. His soft, warm lips brush against mine lightly. I shiver when his hands grip my hips, pulling my body against his. He licks the seam of my mouth, seeking access, and I grant it without hesitation. His tongue dips into me, slow sensual strokes. Deeper. Tasting. Devouring. Claiming. A small whimper escapes, and he swallows it. Our tongues dance in tantalizing movements. I tangle my fingers in his hair. Wanting him against me. Needing him closer.

When he breaks the kiss, I feel the loss. "We better go, Petal, or I will fuck you on my bike." His crude but honest words have my pussy pulsing with an ache that needs to be sated. He readjusts the front of his jeans. The thick, hard ridge behind his zipper has me licking my lips. Every time we're together, it becomes more difficult to let him go. We slip on our helmets and take off down the highway back toward the city.

Fifteen minutes later, we pull up to the house. I pretty much live here now. Being in his home calms me. Even with the flutter of staff and the music, it's homey. As if you are always welcome. No matter who you are or what you do.

The living room is desolate when we step inside. It's so unlike weekdays. I glance into the studio as we pass and notice it's vacant too. Everyone must have gone out. The weather is incredible.

"I guess there's still leftovers. Unless you wanted something else? I'm not sure what's in the fridge." I follow him into the kitchen.

"It's fine. I remember there was pasta salad Ki and I made yesterday."

He nods, opening the silver door and peering inside. "Get plates, baby." Grabbing two plates, I set them on the counter. The large bowl is almost finished. Liam was at it again.

"So, Hayes, do you always take your staff out on romantic balloon trips?" I ask, taking glasses from the overhead cabinet.

"Only the beautiful ones." A mischievous wink in my direction makes me blush.

"Callum . . ."

"Look, Petal." He rounds the counter and saunters up to me. Circling his arms around my hips, he tugs me against his rock-hard body. "I like you. You're gorgeous. You are a sassy little minx. I love your sassy mouth, and I need to be with you." He leans in, his face inches from mine. "I want you. Say yes. You can't tell me you don't feel it. I can see it in your eyes." His warm breath is sweet, and I crave to taste him. I want to respond, but no words come out. "Give us a chance?" The pleading in his eyes tugs at my heart.

My slow nod confirms my agreement. With that, his mouth crashes on mine. His lips are warm and soft. I whimper with a yearning unknown to me. He could bend me over this table right now, and I would comply. My mouth opens to him, giving him access I know he seeks. It's instinctive. I need this, and I need him. Against my better judgment, I let him take me.

His tongue slides in and out, fucking my mouth. The action causing me to squirm, squeezing my thighs together to dull the ache. The kiss is not hurried but slow and sensual. Those strong hands wander to my hips, gripping my ass, hoisting me against him. Placing me on the dinner table, he steps between my legs. I tangle my fingers through his hair, tugging him closer.

A slight moan escapes my lips, and he swallows every whimper. The hard ridge in the front of his pants presses against my pulsing core. A rough growl rumbles in his chest. His hips thrust forward, and his cock rubs against my heated pussy. The aching eases at the contact. I want him inside me. I need him inside me. He steps back and breaks the kiss. "You feel so perfect, Petal. I don't think I could control myself if that happens again." His voice is low, raspy, and filled with need.

"I know. I . . ." Glancing down, heat spreads over my skin. Callum's warm hands cup my face making me look up at him. The soft pads of his thumbs swipe my cheeks softly.

"You're beautiful. We can take it slow. I don't want to scare you off."

"Okay. Slow." I offer him a smile. A noise from the living room startles us, and Callum jumps backward.

"Callum! Are you here?" Kierra calls out.

"In the kitchen."

As soon as she walks in, her face is one of excitement. A smile curves her lips, and she shakes her head in disbelief. "You two sneaky shits." She strides to the fridge, grabbing a bottle of icy water. We both watch her like she's the entertainment.

"What do you want, Kierra?"

"I needed to check on you. Find out how the songs are developing. How are you, Tay?"

"Excellent. I, um . . . Well, Callum and I were just getting something to eat."

"I'm sure you were. Just tidy up when you're done on the table." She offers us both a smirk and makes her way out of the kitchen.

"She took it well." He shrugs and continues to plate our brunch. I can only gape at the handsome rock star standing next to me. I hop off the table, busying myself by grabbing forks. I slip into the chair, speculating what the hell just happened. Callum and I are out. Not in public yet, but Kierra knows. We chat and eat. It's so easy with him. When we finish our salad, he clears our plates and sets them in the dishwasher. I swig down my juice and add my glass to the tray.

"So, is there anything particular you want to do for the day?"

"You could teach me the guitar?" I peer up at his shocked but pleased expression.

"I can do that." With a kiss on the cheek, his hand slides in mine, and he tugs me along with him. We make our way into the studio, closed off from the rest of the house. It's a soundproof room with an old, comfortable sofa. The instruments are all packed away neatly against one wall. The mixing desks are empty of coffee cups and anything else that's normally strewn across them.

"Sit down. Let me play you something first."

Crossing my legs under me, I get comfortable on the couch. He sits on the stool and grabs his guitar. He's directly opposite me, my special VIP experience. People pay hundreds of dollars to see him like this, and here I am about to have a one-on-one acoustic performance. He places the guitar on his thighs, and I am jealous. It's ridiculous, I know, but I can't help it. Then he plays. A few chords. Quick. Soft. I'm transfixed by his fingers, strumming the strings as he tunes by ear. The sound echoes in the modest space.

He cuts a brief glimpse to me. With a wink and smile, he faces down and plays.

My breathing hitches. I don't move. My eyes become glued to him. My heart and mind filled with the haunting melody. His voice crashes over me like a wave, and I am drowning in the lyrics. My favorite song. "Damaged Angel." He's haunted by the lyrics, just as I am. He's not damaged. He's perfect. In every way. When it ends, I'm still. Silent. Afraid to break the spell he's spun. It courses through my veins like the best drug. His glance locks on me. The talent seeps from his pores. I have heard that song hundreds of times, but hearing it played acoustically is an experience I can't begin to explain.

"How was that?" Uncertainty flashed in his gaze, which is unwarranted.

"You reached into my soul. Gripped it, held on, and squeezed until it became unbearable, but blissful. Then you released it, and satisfaction swept over me." The description is straight from my heart. From deep within the darkest part of me. There is no other way to express it.

His expression is melancholy, replacing the guitar on the rack. Rising from the stool, he strides to me on the sofa. Flopping down, he reaches for my hand and draws it up to his mouth. With a gentle, tender kiss on my knuckles, I shiver. Overcome with emotion.

"Come here, Petal." He tugs me over to him. Without thinking, I straddle his lap and grasp his shoulders. Those warm hands find their way under my top, stroking my back. At first, I stiffen. Hopefully, he won't notice how my skin feels under his fingertips. My eyes flutter closed, the sensation of his touch sending heat traveling to my core. My pussy aches and my hips rock against him. "I want to kiss you now." His hoarse murmur brings a smile to my face.

I lean in, and our lips crash together. Our kiss is sweet but gradually becomes more urgent. A growl rumbles in his throat, and I shamelessly rub myself against him. The ridge of his cock strains the front of his pants. His index finger strokes my spine, from my neck down over the tattoo he hasn't yet seen — a shiver racks through my body. I'm not ready for him to see it or the scars. The thought of him pushing me away, the way the others did, constricts my throat. I can't show him. He wouldn't want the broken, damaged woman I am.

His hand drops to the hem of his T-shirt, and he slips it over his head. The magnificently toned body I have seen in so many tabloid photos is in front of me — every ridge and dip of his chiseled torso. His skin is smooth and so silky. Placing my palms flat on his chest, I feel how his skin is smooth and so silky; heat emanates from him. With slow caresses over his skin, I trace lines to his cut obliques that peek at me from his hips. He grunts. "I need to be inside you, Petal. I want to fuck you." The desire dripping from his words pulls at my core. My panties are soaked with arousal for this man.

"I'm not ready. Not right now."

His gaze drops to where our bodies are touching. A throb in his jeans makes the ache between my legs unbearable. "I'll wait for you, Petal." I realize what I can do. What I want to do. The decision in my stare must affirm my intentions. He draws away, and I step back off the sofa. My choice is natural. I drop to my knees, peering up into those stormy, blue eyes. They're dark with hunger. "You don't have—"

"Shh . . ." I make quick work of his belt buckle. Unzipping his pants, I stroke his cock through the thin, black cotton briefs. His head falls back as he hisses my name. Again, and again.

"No. Jesus, Tayla. Stop." His harsh command has me reeling. He sits forward, pulling me up. He pulls his zipper up and tugs me into his arms. "This is not the way I want to do this. I crave you, like nothing I have before, but I need to do it right." His smile is sweet. *He wants a real relationship?*

"But I thought . . ."

"Be with me? Petal, you're incredible. Amazing. Beautiful. Sexy as hell. I can see you. I see through you. Into your heart." His words pierce me deep. "There is nothing more I wish for than to carry you to my bedroom right now. But I will wait till you're ready." Stepping back, he gives me a smile.

"Promise?" I don't know why I need to hear him say it, but I do. The idea of a relationship scares me, but with him, I can try. The public image he portrays isn't the real Callum Hayes. This, right here, is the man I want to know. The one I crave to give myself to. The question remains, will he be able to ignore my scars of the past and accept me for who I am now?

CALLUM

"I promise." I lean in and kiss her again. There's uncertainty in her eyes, and I wonder if it's something I did. My hands roam her curves, lifting the delicate material of her shirt. She is toned, but soft. Supple. My cock is hard. My mouth is watering for her. Without warning, the door behind us swings open. My glance lifts and my blood boils at someone else looking at her body. "Liam. Jesus, can't you knock!" My voice is loud and booms through the small space.

"Well, it's my fucking house too. I can go where I please. What the fuck is going on here?" My brother's stare bounces between Tayla and me. My hands drop, and I tug the hem of her top down, protecting her from his prying eyes.

"I was teaching Tayla the guitar." When I twist to face him entirely, I can see his mind racing through the situation he caught me in only two months previously. I had a groupie in here, and she was riding my dick on the sofa. That didn't end well. Mainly because the poor girl jumped off my lap so fast to cover up, and then when she realized it was my brother, she assumed she struck the jackpot. She wanted a threesome with the Hayes brothers. Unlucky for her, I don't share. Liam pounced on the idea and hauled the little slut out, and I was left wondering what the fuck happened.

"I need to work. Why don't you find another room to have your fun?" His voice is clipped, and I know he doesn't like that somehow Tayla has gotten under my skin. But I'm different with her. We've known each other for a week, and I haven't even gotten into her panties yet. Lacing my fingers through hers, I pull Tay toward the door. As we reach Liam, I lean in and mumble.

"Treat her with the utmost respect, brother." Before he can respond, I stride out with Tayla following behind me. I need to take her to my bedroom, but I don't want her to think I expect anything. "Do you mind going to my room? Or . . .?"

"Sure. I'm sorry your brother was so angry with me being in there. Liam has been amazing this week." We walk to the far end of the house, and I open the door to my bedroom, letting her enter first. With a gentle click, it shuts.

"He's not furious with you, Petal. Liam's annoyed with me. Just ignore him." I watch her eyes take in every inch of my room. My sanctuary. From the black sheets, to the floor to ceiling windows and balcony. I follow her to the window where she's staring at the city beyond with her arms wrapped around her. It's as if she's trying to keep herself together. That if she let's go, she'll break or fall apart.

Stepping up behind her, my arms circle her waist, and I hold her against me. I rest my chin on her shoulder and inhale her sweet perfume. "Callum . . .," she speaks, but as quickly as my lips meet the tender skin on her neck, she trails off. I suck in the delicious taste of her, and her body shudders against me, making my cock hard. Tayla is so beautiful, so responsive. I tighten my hold, needing her closer. Her head drops to the side, granting me access. Taking advantage, I feather kisses from her ear to neck.

As I tug on the neckline of her shirt, she stiffens. "Callum, no." Her tone is forceful, and I step backward. Her eyes latch on mine, and instead of seeing the anger I assumed I would, I see fear.

"What's wrong, Petal? I didn't mean to . . . I . . ."

"It's not you. I . . . There are things you don't know. About me."

"Then tell me?" My stare implores the truth from her. Those chestnut pools glisten with unshed tears, and I want to wrap her in a cocoon and keep her safe. The anxiety is visible in her face, and it tugs on my heart, leaving me breathless. *What the hell has she been through?*

"I can't. Not yet. You'll look at me differently. Can we forget it?" Her gaze drops to her feet, and I take a step toward her. My arms open. She needs to come to me. It has to be her decision.

With a gradual movement, her hungry stare roams up my body. Her eyes are drinking in every inch of me until they lock on mine. A slight smile curls her lips, but it doesn't reach her eyes. There's something she's hiding. I can't force her to reveal it. I can only be here and hope to fuck she tells me soon.

"I am here, Tay, if you ever want to talk. Don't be scared of me." She falls into my arms then, and the contented sigh she exhales doesn't pass unnoticed. Her body shakes, and I realize she's crying. I have only known her for a short time, but I can see behind that tough exterior is someone shattered by memories. Suddenly, she steps back, swiping at her tear-stained cheeks.

"I have to go. Take me home, please?" Up come the walls, and I have no alternative but to surrender to her wishes. "I need space, Callum. I'm sorry." She walks past me, and her perfume washes over me. The soft, sweet scent of fresh apples, reminding me of my childhood. I follow her out of my bedroom, closing the door.

Once we're in the car, she seems to settle down. I'm dying to say something — anything to make her feel better. To reassure her, I will wait. But I'm a pussy when it comes to this girl, so I sit. We drive in silence to her apartment. When I pull up to the curb, she peeks at me through her thick eyelashes. Her hand touches on my knee, sending a jolt of pleasure through my body. "I'm really sorry." Her whisper is filled with worry.

I nod. Watching her get out of my car, it

takes every ounce of my strength to resist going after her. My stare doesn't leave her until she's stepped inside and disappeared. That's when I tear my glare from the emptiness and frown at the road ahead of me. My hands clutch the steering wheel so tight I'm positive it will shatter.

She fucking walked away. From me. Callum fucking Hayes. The tortured expression on her face is seared behind my eyelids. Fuck this. Opening the door of my Jeep, I hop out and round the front. I bound up the stairs to her building. As I reach the entrance, the gate opens. An old lady smiles up at me. "Afternoon, ma'am. I am here to see my girlfriend. Do you mind if I go inside, please?"

She beams at me. "You're a naughty fellow. Always bring flowers. You're forgiven this time." She chuckles and lets me past her.

"I promise to remember that next time." I offer her a wink, and she shuffles off. Running up the stairs, I reach Tayla's door. I inhale a heavy breath, leaning my head against the entrance to my girl's apartment. With my eyes closed, I knock twice.

"Who's there?" Her voice is quiet, gentle. The pain is gone, but she's wary now.

"Open the door Tayla."

"Cal, just go home. Please?"

"I will talk to the door, Tay, but I'm not leaving. Your neighbors may not want to listen to this. But they will if you don't open this goddamn door, woman." My tone is rough but low, and I know she can hear me. I'm not giving up on her. There's something wrong. I can be a dick. This time, it's different. I'm choosing to be a gentleman. Fuck it, Liam was right. I'm going soft.

The click of a lock makes me smile. With a creak, the door opens, her big brown eyes peering up at me. She opens it farther, allowing me inside. As soon as I step through the door, I'm assaulted with her scent. It's so fucking incredible. I can't help moaning.

"What do you want?" Her question catches me off guard. With my back to her, I fist my hands to keep from grabbing her, slamming her against the living room wall, and devouring her.

"You."

One word.

No explanation.

Just her. The gasp behind me is a delicious sound.

"This is—"

"Petal, if I look you in the eye and you give me an excuse for why I shouldn't be here, then I'll lose it. So, when I turn around, you need to accept that no matter what happened, I'm not going anywhere." She's silent for a beat, and I spin on my heel. Her gaze is latched on my movement. I take a step forward; she takes one backward. Fuck, this woman will be the death of me. I advance again, and she steps back. With her body now flush with the wall, she has nowhere to go. I press a hand to either side of her head, caging her in.

Her soft breath hitches and I inhale her scent. My cock is rock hard behind my zipper, and I'm hanging on by a thread. "You, sweet Petal, will not push me aside. I always, and I mean always, get what I want. Now, tell me."

She raises her chin in defiance and glowers at me. "I'm not one of your damn groupies, Callum. You can't deal with me like one. You can't come storming in here demanding me to bend to your will. Just because Callum fucking Hayes wants me to doesn't mean I have to." Her voice is loud, and suddenly I don't care what the fuck she's saying. I grasp her shoulders, haul her against me, and my lips crash down on hers. She tries punching my chest, but I draw her nearer, and my tongue plunges into her mouth with unrelenting force, and she surrenders. All the fight is gone, and she molds to me. She's made to fit next to me.

Her fingers tangle in my unruly hair and pull me closer. The electric current shooting between us is tangible. When our bodies move together, it sparks like lightning during a storm. My blood is on fire, coursing through my veins with need and lust for her. My hands travel down her back, and she shivers. Once I reach her sweet, pert little ass, I grip it, lifting her against my body. I realize she can feel my erection. Her legs wrap around my waist, and I carry her to the sofa.

Without breaking our connection, I lay her down tenderly. I trail up her body, nudging her top up until I find the thin material of her bra. Another growl rumbles in my throat, and she whimpers into my mouth. Her hips lift toward me, and I notice my girl is letting me in.

Her hands are on my chest, pushing gently. "Callum." She breathes my name. I break the kiss, but I don't move. "I am sorry for running. If this is your choice, to be with me, we have to talk." Her voice a low murmur. There's a soft rasp to it, and I know it's because she's turned on.

"Do we have to talk now?" I chuckle, pressing my erection into her, showing her why I don't want to talk. The soft whimper from her tells me she would rather do something else. Without another word, she reaches for my belt. "Petal." She shakes her head, silencing me. I sit back and watch her. The grin she offers is wicked. "No." My tone is harsher than I want, but I'm so turned on I won't last much longer. She peers up at me. The challenge in those chestnut eyes begs me to stop her. "I need to do this right." Scooping her up, I walk into her bedroom. Gently laying her on the bed, I straighten and pull the T-shirt up and off, dropping it on the floor.

Her hungry stare heats my skin. "Your turn, Angel." As she pulls her top off, her long blonde hair tumbles over her breasts and back. I pull my boots off, then my socks. When my jeans drop, I peer up at her. I'm standing in front of her in only my black briefs. A smirk tugs the side of her mouth. "What?"

Her lips part and I hear the sigh as her gaze rakes over me. "You are sort of beautiful." I chuckle at her confession.

"Only sort of?" She nods. I point to her pants. "Off." She complies and unbuttons and tugs them down her smooth, silky legs. As she leans backward, my cock throbs. I can't get any harder. "Fuck." She's wearing bright pink, silk panties with lace edges. Her bra is the same color, and it offsets her creamy complexion perfectly.

"You don't like it?" The apprehension in her tone gets my attention, and I frown.

"Petal, you're perfect." Her body trembles at my words, and I can't help wondering why.

"I'm not perfect. Nobody is." I lean forward and kiss her plump, rose-colored lips. They're swollen and bruised from our earlier kiss.

"Shh . . ." I kneel beside her and plant kisses over her chest lightly, then leisurely to her toned stomach. She has a tattoo running from one hip to the other just below her belly button. *"No longer fragile, but still a Damaged Angel."* "Tayla." My eyes latch onto hers, and I see the tears brimming. Without question, I brush my lips along the ink. Whatever they mean to her, I will know soon enough. I hope. Her little pussy smells incredible. "Jesus, you smell so good."

When I cut a glimpse at her, she's blushing. She's so beautiful it hurts to look at her. I make quick work of her bra. Her breasts are round, heavy, and her pink nipples are tight with arousal. My mouth is watering to taste her. And I do. Lapping at her left nipple, my fingers find the other. She moans her approval of my attention on the hardened buds. My mouth moves to the right pebble, and I lave at it, tasting her sweetness. I pull myself away and hook my thumbs into the waistband of her panties. Once they're on the floor, I hold both her ankles. I feather kisses from her feet up to her knees. The goosebumps that rise on her skin have me grinning. She's as affected by me as I am by her. "Callum." My name on her lips is a soft, pleading whimper.

"Yes, Petal?" My lips dance on the delicate skin of her inner thighs, and she squirms. Her back arching up toward me.

"Please?"

"Please, what? Tell me. I want to hear what you need."

"You." Rising, I shed my boxers, and her eyes are large with surprise. My thick, hard cock is jutting out, pointing to the person I crave more than anything. Tayla. My precious Petal. I kneel between her splayed thighs again, blowing hot breath just below the tattoo on her belly, and drifting down to the entrance of her tight body. Perfect. The muscles in her stomach are taut and sexy. Her legs are beautifully firm. With a tender kiss on her slick little pussy, she cries out my name. It's music to my ears.

My tongue flattens against her bare lips, and I lap at her wet, pink flesh. So sweet, and all fucking mine. With my thumbs, I open her, my flower. Her sopping cunt glistens with arousal.

Open to my gaze. My dick jumps, imploring me to drive into her heat. I bring my mouth down on her clit, suckling it. She fists my hair, tugging me closer as her body writhes and bucks against me.

My two fingers slip inside her tight, molten pussy, and she flies over the edge — her core pulsing around my digits. I suck and lick her until she gradually comes down from her high. The incredible nectar of her release is a drug. I can never get enough of her. My eyes shoot up, and I take in the rosy glow on her cheeks. The small smirk curving her plump mouth is heaven. Perfect. "Now, I'm going to fuck you."

She gasps at my words. I snatch the foil packet and rip it open. Sheathing my shaft, I crawl over her. When the tip nudges her pussy, she raises her hips, and I groan. I grit my teeth, forcing myself to go slow. The speed is torturous, but I don't want to hurt her. Her eyes are wide as she stares at me. "Fuck me, Callum. Hard." Her raspy voice is laden with desire. That's all the permission I need. Without another warning, I slam into her. "Callum!" Her scream is loud, and her nails dig into my shoulders. I pull out and drive back in. "Yes." Her low hiss in my ear spurs me on, and I pound into her.

Her legs wrap around my waist, pulling me in deeper. Fuck, this woman is perfect. She fits me like a glove. My cock is so deep inside her. I draw out and plunge to the hilt, into her tight little cunt. Her breathless moans are beautiful.

My orgasm shoots down my spine. "Come with me, Petal, all over my dick." Her body stiffens and pulses around me. Milking my release from me. Our bodies are moving simultaneously. We're connected, body, mind, and soul. As soon as she screams my name, I growl hers as we meet sweet oblivion together.

TAYLA

I wake with a start. My mind is foggy. It's dark, and I can't fathom why. *Did I oversleep?* My body is heavy. Then I realize there is someone behind me. Memories of earlier today flit through my thoughts, and I remember Callum. After we made love, we passed out. Rolling over, I glance at the magnificent man asleep. *Shit!* I'm naked. *Fuck, fuck, fuck!* I swing my legs over the bed, careful not to wake him. I snatch my bathrobe and pull it on. My heart is racing. *Did he see?* He couldn't have. There's no way he wouldn't demand an explanation if he did.

Taking a deep, calming breath, I pad into the bathroom. I grimace at my appearance in the mirror. My reflection is scary. I look like I've been dragged through a bush. My eyes are puffy and red. I splash cold water on my face and give it a quick dab with a towel. Back in the bedroom, I find him rolled over onto my side of the bed. He's hugging my pillow with his nose buried in the soft cotton. Almost as if he was inhaling my scent.

"Don't just stand there." The low, gravelly voice millions of women love beckons me, and I giggle. Walking over to him, I kneel on the edge. My gaze drinks in his beautifully tanned skin and inked, toned arms. The muscles of his exposed torso under the dim light shining through the window makes him ethereal.

"I assumed you and the pillow wanted some alone time." His sky-blue pools dart open, staring at me with a mischievous glint.

"I would prefer alone time with you, Petal." I lean forward and plant a tender kiss on his cheek. There is a tousle-haired rock god sprawled naked in my sheets, and I need to take advantage of that, but I'm starving.

"I'm hungry. Feed me if you want more than a quiet night in." As he sits up, the sheet falls from his stomach, and his chiseled abs are on display to my eager gaze. God, he's magnificent.

"And what would my angel like to eat?" The word angel sinks into my heart. His smile is sweet. The look in his eyes has my heart racing.

"Not sure. I'll make coffee first." I turn, leaving him in bed. In the kitchen, I turn on the kettle and grab two mugs from the cupboard. I feel him behind me. When I turn, I find him wrapped in a towel, hung low on his taut hips. Like a predator, he stalks toward me. The smirk on his lips is wicked and sends a tingle through me. He's beautifully inked as tattoos adorn his arms, and one weaves over his chest.

"I'm hungry right now." The low timbre of

his voice has my knees wobbling.

"Behave yourself, Hayes. We need to eat."

He cages me against the counter with both his arms. He leans in and murmurs in my ear, "I would love to eat . . ." His warm breath fans over my neck and goosebumps rise over every inch of my body. "Your delectable, wet, tight little pussy." I gasp. His hands make quick work of my robe, and as it pools to my feet, Callum drops to his knees. I look down into steel-blue eyes that stare up at me like I'm his last meal on earth. He leans forward, his nose against my skin as he inhales — from my knee up to my inner thigh — at a slow, deliberate pace. *Holy fuck!* My knees buckle, and his hands reach up to grasp my hips, holding me up against the counter.

Once his nose reaches my core, a deep rumble in his chest tells me dinner may still be a little while. "Spread your legs, Petal." I comply, opening my limbs to his greedy gaze. My grip on the countertop is tight. Callum's tongue slowly teases the hypersensitive skin on my inner thigh. Close, but not close enough. Teasing. Moving his attention to my other leg, he does the same. My knees are weak, and I'm not sure I can hold myself up any longer. His grip tightens on my hips. My body is pressed painfully against the granite behind me. His tongue lands flat on my molten core.

He suckles my bare lips into his hot mouth, his tongue flicking over my bundle of nerves that ache for relief. Another long lick, and I cry out. My release is close. With his slow expert movements, my body is a volcano ready to erupt. The knot in my belly tightens, and I can't think straight. All that matters is the orgasm Callum is about to unleash on me.

His two fingers slide into my tight heat, sending me spiraling out of control. He crooks both digits, hitting my sweet spot. I feel his hand move as stars explode behind my eyelids, and somewhere in my mind, I'm screaming and mewling. His name is a chant on my lips as my body shudders. He brings one hand to my leg, and the other still has a vice-like grip on my hip. My knees give out, but he catches me, holding me against him. A shuddering aftershock of my orgasm rips into me, and I collapse in his arms. "God . . ." My voice is so rough and raspy.

"I have been called that once or twice." With a mischievous wink, his eyes sparkle with mischief. I swat him playfully.

"Don't be an ass." His hands slowly stroke my back, and the realization hits me he will feel the scars. *Shit!* Jumping up, I grasp my robe and tug it on.

"Petal? What's wrong?" The concern in his gaze unnerves me.

I can't do this.

I can't do this.

He can't know.

"Nothing. Do you want coffee?"

"No. What the fuck just happened?" Spinning on my heel, I scoot past him out of the kitchen and into the living room. I curl myself on the sofa, with my head on my knees, inhaling short deep breaths.

I can't do this.

I can't do this.

The mantra playing in my mind numbs me. I can't think. Thoughts of him finding out the truth about my past and leaving tear me apart. "Jesus, Tayla. Talk to me, baby."

He perches next to me, encircling me, and my whole body goes rigid. With slow strokes over my back, his touch calms my heart rate. My breathing evens, and I steal a glance at him. "Callum, you called me a damaged angel earlier."

"No, angel. You're not damaged." The tears that were threatening spill as I blink and nod quickly.

"I am. So fucking broken you don't realize."

"Then enlighten me, Petal. It kills me to see you so hurt." Our eyes lock for an eternity. There's something in his expression. Inside the blue depths, trust fills me, like an empty cup. No one has seen this part of me, and if they did, they'd run. I chose a relationship with Callum. I'll have to show him. To tell him. The thought terrifies me shitless, but I don't have a choice.

"I want you to promise me that no matter what I say, you won't judge me." His eyebrows crease in confusion. "You also need to let me finish before you respond. Before you walk away and never come back, give me a chance to tell my story."

"I'm not leaving, Tayla. Talk." My heart is sputtering in my rib cage. It might force its way out of my chest before I get everything out. I drop my feet to the floor and stand in front of him. My lips purse in a harsh line. I don't meet his passionate stare. I loosen the sash of the robe, letting it slide over my shoulders and pool on the carpet.

"If you're trying to tell me something awful, this isn't helping." The wicked smirk he gives almost makes me smile, but I put a finger on my lips; gesturing for him to shush.

I lift my hair, twirling it up onto my head. As soon as I turn around, the audible gasp that rushes from him has me cringing. He's silent. Painfully silent. My body shudders. Fear wrenches in my chest. My heart wringing with the ache of him leaving. The heat from his naked chest at my back is unexpected. I can sense it. He's not touching me. I didn't expect him to want to put his hands on me. The sadness in my heart is worse than the agony of what happened.

You're a disgusting little slut. Do you hear me? Nobody will ever want you. Just remember who did this to you. This is what you deserve. Teasing me for months. This will make sure you're never going to tease another man again. They will look at you with disgust because you're filthy. If only your daddy knew what a little whore you are. If you ever tell him it was me, I will find your sister and take her too. Do you hear me?

The voice invades my mind. I squeeze my eyes shut, blocking it out. I draw a deep breath and speak again. "So. I, uhm . . ." Dropping my hair, I shift back to him, and the rage in his stare is unmistakable. He is radiating anger, and I clutch my robe. "That's what you touched. A monster. I'm ruined, Callum." My tone is sharp. The wince is obvious on his face. I spin on my heel and run into my bedroom.

"Tayla, don't walk away from me. Please? I'm not fucking leaving. You need to tell me what the fuck happened. What disgusting piece of shit could do this to you, baby?" The pain in his tone rips my heart in two. *How can he be standing here?*

I sense his presence behind me. The heat of his body against mine. "I saw the horror and disgust in your eyes." The tears I held onto spill down my cheeks. I step up to the large window. I can't face him, so the next best thing is to look outside. Anywhere but at the distaste in his expression. I know it's there. They all look at me the same way. He made sure of that.

"It was a few years ago. I've told no one — not even my sister. I was ashamed of my choices. This . . . is my burden to bear. My mistake. I chose the wrong path in my life, and I paid for it." My voice cracks with emotion. "He assured me no man could ever want me." When Callum's hand settles on my shoulder, I start. The touch is so light, but the air is heavy between us.

"Well, he fucked up." His tone is rough and

gentle in my ear. *What?* I whirl around and peer at him. Those blue pools that earlier held fear and rage in them have something else. Not love, but an emotion close to it, and it suffocates me.

"What do you mean?" It's my turn to frown at him.

"I want you. But I need you to be honest. What happened? And where is this fucking asshole? I want to fuck him up so bad the dick will never walk again." His body shudders with anger. There is vengeance in his stance. I don't doubt he would do it. Shaking my head, I turn back to face the city below.

"He's gone. They arrested him. Apparently, I wasn't the first victim. Why are you still here?" I meet those cerulean pools. The sincerity in his gaze is filled with awe. But I am flawed. Broken. There is nothing worth wanting. His arms encircle my waist and hold me against him.

"You, Petal. Are perfect. I choose to be here. Do you trust me to tell me the rest?" He's only wearing a towel, and I'm too aware of his thickness pressing against my ass. I step away, making myself comfortable on the bench seat at the window.

"I'd just turned eighteen. I was staying with a friend. My father, he managed to pay for my studies, but he couldn't afford a dorm for me. The thing is, he lost his fortune because of his business associate. The police couldn't recover what was lost. We didn't have anything. I didn't have anything." Drawing a deep breath,

I continue, all the while facing outside. "I had to work. My classmate told me about a job she had. Said she made enough money to pay for her own off-campus apartment. All I had to do was dance." His breathing hitches.

"Not stripping. Aerial dancing is a form of fitness. Where I have bands of material fastened to the ceiling, and I twist and twirl in the air. I didn't strip. Since I did it to keep fit, I didn't see an issue with it. It was something fascinating to watch." Cal sits opposite me, his hand on my knee. The pad of his thumb strokes circles on my skin. Tears spill down my cheeks, and I swipe them away. "That's when he saw me and recognized my face. He was older, thirty-five. I was young and stupid. He was my father's business partner. He evaded the police until he landed in the club where I was working. Threatening to expose me to my parents, he forced me to go home with him. I was so stupid. I was afraid to go to the police. He started out pushing me around, telling me . . ."

A sob cracks my voice, and I shiver. "He told me I'm worthless. One night, he came to my place drunk. We argued because I told him I couldn't do it anymore." Callum pulls me against him. I clamber into his lap, taking comfort in his embrace. "He took out a blade, forced me to lie on a table. Then he tied me to it. I couldn't move. He . . ." I swallow the emotion thick in my throat. Callum's body stiffens, and the rhythm of his heart speeds up. "He ripped my top off; sliced rather, and my bra along with it. Then he marked my back. So I could never dance again. He said it was my fault. I was teasing him. Making men . . ." My words taper into silence. The vibration of anger flowing from Callum is evident. It fills the air between us.

"Shh, baby." Pulling me to stand, he positions me between his legs. His fingers tug my bathrobe, and it falls open. Feathering kisses on my belly, he grips my hips, holding me steady. He rises, and our bodies are flush. A slight nudge and the silky material slips over my shoulders and pools at my feet. This is the first time anyone has exposed me this way. Not my body, but my soul. He has taken my pain, my aching heart, and splayed it to his gaze. "Pull your hair to the side." Callum's voice is tender. Caring. Calming. My desire to comply is overwhelming. I obey his order, watching him move around me. Once he steps behind me, I'm not scared any longer. His lips on me send an unusual awareness through me. *He's falling for me too.* The soft, feather-light kisses over my back, on each part of my tattoo, have goosebumps rising on my skin — from the top of my shoulder blades down to my ass. When he's done, having placed a kiss on every inch of my inked skin, he turns me to look at him. Strong, loving hands frame my face, and the pads of his thumbs swipe my cheeks. All the emotion I've kept bottled up shatters and explodes.

"Handsome, I have no clue how to be in a

relationship." The smile he gives me is serious and beautiful all at the same time. "He ruined me. Earlier, when we had sex. That was the first time I trusted someone to . . . Touch me." The harsh truth of my words shocks him and me. We stare at each other for a moment.

"Neither do I. We are in new territory, and all I want to do is be near you. My life is intense, Petal. It's public, and if you can't deal with that, then we'll find a way past that. I need you. I do. Every exquisite inch of you. You're so far from ruined. I see you as incredible and strong, and you're mine." His confession seeps into me, into my veins, into my cracked soul. And I knew it would soon drench my heart.

"Callum, it will be difficult. I mean, I can't walk away from you right now." My eyes lock on his, showing him through my gaze that my feelings run deeper than we both thought.

"I realize the tabloids paint me as a heartless dick, but I'm not. There are things I'm not proud of doing, but if you agree, we can figure it out." Without another word, I wrap my arms around him. I need his warmth. He leans in and whispers in my ear, "Besides, you have the most delicious little pussy I have ever felt. Like you were made for me." That earns him a giggle.

"You're so romantic, Hayes." He shrugs and wipes my wet cheeks and whispers a kiss on my forehead.

"I never claimed to be less than perfect."

"Thank you, Cal, for not . . . I don't know.

For not leaving."

"Don't thank me. You're everything I could ever want. And I'm not losing you."

My rock star is perfect. He's the man who kissed my scars that are concealed by the tattoo. He picks me up and walks to the bed. Dinner forgotten. Laying me down, he spoons against me. My eyes close as he envelops me. My body against his, the heat of his chest against my back.

Sleep welcomes me, and then the nightmare shows up.

"Little angel, see how elegant you are? Do you realize that you're mine? There will never be another man in your life. Do you know how I figure that? Because I will make sure of it. Do you understand me, you filthy slut?" My muscles are weakening. I have no idea what he injected into me, but there's fire in my veins. I'm sprawled on a table, my arms and legs shackled, and the icy steel gouges into my back. It's not as unpleasant as the substance he shot into me. "My sexy dancing bitch. That's what you are. Twirling and swinging around on those harnesses." The sting of pain bites as he teases my skin with the blade.

"Please, I will do anything. Let me go? I have to get home tonight. I can't stay here. My family, they'll be looking for me." A second blinding slice in my skin, and I cry out in anguish.

"You will leave when I allow you to." His thick, rough fingers caress the entrance to my body, and the torment blinds me instantly. "You love it, don't you? Your little sister will be mine too."

"No! You can't touch her. Take me. Leave her

alone." My begging is what he loves.
The pleading.
The crying.
The trembling.
He gets off on it.
"Oh, I'm taking your little cunt, then hers. So sweet. Wherever you go, you will remember me."

CALLUM

Since Tayla told me about what happened to her, I've been glued to her side. The fact that she works with me makes it easier, so I can check up on her. Her nightmares started, and even though she assures me she's okay, the fear I saw in her eyes that first night I woke her ripped me in two. Ever since, she hasn't left my sight. If I'm not here, Liam and Ryan are. My heart is in this. I doubt she'll leave or hurt me. Still, I'm terrified of losing her.

We head to the airport tomorrow. Paparazzi will hound us at every stop. We've been together for a month, but it's still been kept quiet. I didn't want her to be the focus of the cameras until she needs to be. So, I had to behave myself around her in public. "Hayes!" I realize I'm in shit when she calls me by my last name. I chuckle because she's so damn cute when she's angry.

"In here."

"What the fuck were you doing yesterday?" She storms into my bedroom, and I have no idea what's gotten into her now. Slapping the paper on the bed next to me, I glance down. My eyes scan the story. I was caught on camera in Agent Provocateur. "Can you explain what you were doing there?"

"I was buying you a birthday present, if you must know. It was a gift for me too, and I can't wait to unwrap it." My grin earns me a huff, but her resolve crumbles.

"Goddamnit. You're infuriating."

"That's why we have such incredible sex. Make-up sex is the best. Didn't you know?" I draw her into me. She's standing between my thighs, and I peer up into those beautiful, shiny, chestnut eyes. "Kiss me." When she leans down, I realize her anger has dissipated. Her lips find mine in a gentle, tender kiss, but I need more. I lie back and pull her down on top of me, allowing her to straddle me.

"Guys! Get a room." Liam leans against the doorjamb. My brother has been giving me grief since Tayla moved in.

"We are in a room. Mine. Now get the fuck out."

"Pizza's here. Better grab yours before it disappears." He turns and leaves us alone. Another soft kiss and Tay jumps off me and pulls her flowing blonde hair into a messy bun.

"Come on. I'm hungry. And I want my present early." She winks and walks out of my room with a sway in her sexy hips. The day we play Wembley is her birthday. I'll never forget June eleventh for as long as I live.

After dinner, we sat down to talk about the schedule. We needed to make sure everything was packed. Most of the equipment is delivered to the venues or brought in, but the critical instruments we will take on the flight tomorrow. Tayla left us to take a shower. As I stroll into my bedroom, I find it empty. "Tay?"

"Bathroom." Wandering over to the *en suite*, I lean against the doorjamb, staring at the most exquisite woman I have ever laid eyes on. Her long hair is wrapped in a towel, and she has one of my cutout tanks on. The pattern is perfect because the curve of her gorgeous tits is visible. My cock jumps at the view. Her tattoo weaves over her ribs, and I detest the artist who got to ink her there.

"This is how I should be welcomed home daily." Her blush is evident as it spreads from her cheeks to her chest. Stepping into the bathroom, I watch her moisturize her face. I circle my arms around her waist. Her soft, supple skin under my lips begs to be licked, devoured. I plant kisses from her neck to her shoulder. The need to taste her overtakes me, and I suck her sweet, silky flesh into my mouth.

"I'm sure that could be arranged, Mr. Hayes. Any other demands?" Her sassy mouth is in full force tonight, and I have plans for it. I lean in and bite her earlobe, earning me a sexy whimper.

"In fact, now that you mention it. I do. I want you on my bed in five minutes. Naked. Spread open and waiting." With a swat on her pert little ass, she yelps and runs into the bedroom. I drag my tank up over my head and unbutton my jeans. The zipper is half down. They hang off my hips, just the way I know she loves. Nothing can prepare me for what I see when I walk into the bedroom. *Fuck!*

She's on my black sheets on her back, her smooth legs splayed wide and her hair loose on the pillow. Her body is bare of any clothes, and her eyes are sparkling with desire. "Now this . . . right here . . . is how I demand to be greeted every day." I lean forward and kiss her. It's a chaste peck which takes all my restraint. "Rollover." Without hesitation, she rolls onto her stomach. I grab the oils I bought two days ago and squirt the lavender-scented oil onto her skin in a pattern that matches the vines running the length of her back. Even though her tattoo covers the scars, I know they're there. She was frightened I would freak out when I saw them, and that they made her hideous. I think they make her more beautiful. They reveal her strength.

There is something between us I've never felt with anyone before. When we make love, our souls unite in a melody fit for heaven. The damaged angel, as she loves to call herself, is the heaven to my hell. I wish she could understand how beautiful she is. I want her to see what

I do. Perfection in the purest form. She's been dragged through hell, but her wings are still white as snow.

All the lyrics that occupied my mind in recent weeks have been about her. Every time I sit to compose, the words are about her. What she makes me feel. I massage the oil into her skin. The tattoo glistening. An intricate design. Vines and cherry blossoms intertwine, covering the lefthand side of her body. The other side is an angel wing. At the tip of the wing are flames that are about to engulf it. And in between the vines are shattered hearts, between love and fire. That's perfect. I should write that down, but nothing will pull me away from her right now. Underneath the ink are the small scars that dot her back. Incisions made with a knife.

My hands move over her, and the sweet-scented lotion makes her smooth and silky. "Callum, can we make love now?" I didn't realize I had been sitting here, staring at her for fifteen minutes. Her head turns. She's facing me, and I grin, nodding.

"You don't have to ask me twice." I lean forward and kiss her. Then I nudge my jeans off. I'm rock hard for my girl. Turning her over, I shift between her splayed thighs. Our lips meet, and when she opens for me, my tongue licks into her. It's a quick, luscious kiss I have to break. I sit back and reach over to the nightstand, snatching a condom. Her eyes follow my every move. When I grip my throbbing shaft, her gaze is glued to the sight. She watches me stroke myself. "Is this what you want, Petal?" Her tongue flicks out, moistening her lips, and I can no longer hold back. I ache for her. Her nod is swift, and I need no other confirmation.

I sheath my cock and slide over her gorgeous body, the tip of my erection nudging her pussy. "Please, Callum." She will be my undoing. I reach between us and stroke her slick cunt. So fucking wet for me. She's always ready for me. Without warning, I slam into her — all the way to the hilt. Her beautiful cries are music to my ears. Our bodies move in the rhythm of our love song. When we make love, fuck, have sex, I feel alive. Complete. Euphoric.

Her legs wrap around my waist, tightening, drawing me in farther. Her tight, hot pussy pulses around me. I ease out and tease her again. "Callum, stop teasing, just fuck me." *Mmm, you want it hard, Petal? Fine.* I sit back, and she whimpers at the loss of me.

"On your knees." Her gaze widens, but she immediately moves onto all fours. "Good girl." I drive into her, fast and deep. Her moans spurring my thrusts. I fist her long golden hair in my hand and tug her head backward. In response, her cunt tightens and squeezes my shaft. I rain a slap down on her pert little ass, and she yelps — such a provocative sound.

My body drives into hers, deeper, hitting her sweet spot. I pull out slowly and thrust back in. Over and over again. Her body is warm, taking me. Every inch. Accepting me. The sweat that sheens her skin is beautiful, as if she's glistening. When her pussy tightens around me, I realize she's close. As her body shudders with release, she cries out my name. My body stiffens, and my cock thickens. Filling the condom with a growl of her name on my lips. We collapse on the bed. After discarding the rubber, I drape my arm over her, holding her against me. She smells of sex and cherries. It's a heady combination.

"That was incredible." She turns over in my arms, facing me. Her eyes are glossy. She has a freshly fucked glow in her cheeks, and I must be honest. It suits her. After the number of women I've fucked, she's the only one I can also make love to.

The sun flooding through the open blinds is too bright. Today will be a long day. The flight is a good twelve hours. Rolling over, I find my lovely blonde girl sitting at the window. Her hair is loose, and she's wrapped up in a blanket, and I have a feeling nothing else. Her knees are drawn up to her chin. She's calm. After watching her for a while, I sit up. "Are you okay, Petal?" When she twists, her smile is small, and I recognize something is wrong.

"Just thinking about the next few months. The days and nights will be crazy." I nod and swing my feet over the edge of the bed.

"It will be. Are you sure you're ready?" She nods, and I notice the uncertainty in her features.

"I want to come with you. I do." Her voice is soft, but she's made up her mind. With the sheet around my waist, I pad over to her.

"You are safe with us. We have security that monitors everyone who comes to the venue." I stand in front of her. Doe eyes peer up at me. When the wicked smirk curls her lips, I realize I'm in for a morning treat. She slips from the chair and sinks to her knees. With a rough tug, she pulls the sheet from me. "Baby . . ." The words trail off as her mouth opens. Her tongue darts out and runs over the tip of my cock.

A small moan in her chest sends a jolt through me. I watch her plump lips slide down my thick shaft, and her eyes peer up at me. They're shining with mischief. The tip hits the back of her throat, and she swallows. The sensation tightens my balls, and my head drops in satisfaction. "Shit, woman, you feel incredible." My voice is a rough rumble. Her hands clutch my thighs, and my hand fists in her long, ice-blonde hair. I hold her still, reveling in the feel of her. She moans, the sensation sending vibrations over my shaft. Then I fuck her mouth, drawing my pleasure from her. "I will come, baby, you better stop now." She ignores me and flicks her tongue around my cock. She opens her jaw, and I'm so deep inside her that her nose is against my abs. Taking all nine inches into her mouth. None of the women I've been with have ever been able to do that. My release shoots down my spine into my dick and spurts into her waiting throat. She doesn't spill a drop of my hot seed. I slip out from between her lips, and she licks me clean. The innocence in her face after what she did has my mind spinning with all the dirty things I ache to do to her.

"You will kill me if you do that every day."

Her sweet giggle echoes through my foggy mind. "I didn't hear you complaining when I was doing it." Rising, she leans up on her tiptoes and presses a kiss on my cheek. She spins, drops the blanket, and strolls into the bathroom. Before the door closes, she glances back with an invitation I would be foolish to ignore her.

So, like any sensible man would, I follow her. Her cherry body wash is on the shelf. I snatch it and lather up the cloth. Taking my time, I wash her gently. Her skin looks so delicate, wet, and gleaming. In slow, circular motion, I massage her body. Then I sink to my knees. My hands drift down her legs, kneading. The soft moans from her have my cock hard again. I need to be inside her. I straighten and rinse her off. With my hand in hers, I pull her from the shower. She stares at my reflection as I quickly towel dry her. I make quick work of drying my body. "Hold onto the counter, baby; don't move." In the bedroom, I grab a condom and roll it on. When I join her again, I find her bent at the waist. I step behind her. My fingers tease her slick folds. Our eyes lock in the mirror, and the desire in her gaze is almost my undoing. I slowly inch into her tight pussy.

The movement has her pushing back against me, but I grip her hips and hold her still. "Open your eyes. Watch me. Look at me fuck your flawless body." Dark brown pools lock on my blue ones in the mirror. Her lips part as whimpers and moans escape her. I plunge into her, pressing her against the counter. With my hand gripping her hip, the other strokes her spine, tracing soft lines along the tattoo. Over her scars. My hips move back and then drive forward, taking her sweet, beautiful pussy. Her hands claw at the counter, but my movements speed up, and she can't grip anything. "You see how beautiful you are, with my cock inside your tight pussy?"

"Cal . . . please?" I know she's needing release. I reach forward and strum her hardened nub, which has her flying over the edge. Her body tightens around me, pulling me into her. As her orgasm splinters through her, a growl so primal shudders in my chest. Slipping out as she rides her high. I slide my fingers into her pulsing pink flesh. She's tight, dripping, and the scent of her arousal has my cock thickening with release. I pull off the rubber and shoot my seed over her inked skin.

"Now I've marked you. You are mine." An easy smile appears, but it doesn't reach her chestnut eyes. "Did I hurt you?"

"No. I don't like when you're not inside me."

Her cheeks pink with embarrassment. Once the condom is in the trash, I grab a towel and clean her skin. She turns to me, and I cup her face in my hands and kiss her.

"You're beautiful. Can I ask you something?" She nods, but she's wary. "Why only one wing? And why cherry blossoms? I've been wondering since you showed me."

"One means I'm broken, damaged. But cherry blossoms are a promise of something beautiful. Delicate." Her gaze drops to her feet. She's open, letting me in and the moment pulls at my heart. Deep down, I realize I'm falling for her, and there's nothing I can do to stop it.

"You will never be damaged again. And you're beautiful." I make her a promise I intend to keep. The tour will be a test of our relationship. Groupies. Models. And all I want to do is shelter her from it, but I know I can't. I want no one but her. Still, I have a terrible feeling. And that scares me shitless.

TAYLA

We're in the car on our way to the airport. I'm tired, but the excitement overshadows it. I get to see my sister for my birthday, which will be fun. Pulling my phone from my purse, I open my Twitter account. Social media has blown up since the tour was announced. I'm now publicly revealed as part of the crew. So I have more notifications than I can handle. Scrolling through my feed, I spot a picture that sends jealousy coursing through my veins. My body stiffens, and I know Callum feels it. We're sitting close enough that our arms are touching.

"You okay, baby?" His voice in my ear sends shivers down my spine. I shake my head. As I turn the screen, the photo is open, and his eyes bulge. Him and Arina. His ex-girlfriend. "Fuck." The curse a low hiss.

"How old is this picture?" I glare at him. There's something in his expression that confirms it was recent. My heart constricts. My throat closes, and dizziness sweeps over me. Anger fuels me, and the ache in my chest leaves me breathless.

"About two weeks." Just then, our driver pulls up to the airport. I snatch my bag and open the door. Before he says anything more, I jump out of the SUV. I hear him call after me but ignore it, making my way toward the departures lounge through the hordes of people. It's busy, so I weave between families and couples. Before I reach the VIP area, Callum's hand clutches my arm. Spinning me around, his eyes find mine.

"Let. Me. Go." My tone is filled with venom.

"I will not let you go. This is ludicrous. I need to explain."

"No. You don't get that chance. You lost that right when you hid me in the back of the car every time we went anywhere in public. I'm not a fucking dirty little secret you take out when it's convenient for you. How long have you been seeing her?" This is the first photo I've seen on any social media with him and her since they ended things a year ago.

"Would you calm down and listen?" He pulls the hood of his sweatshirt over his head. I glance around and realize stragglers have now stopped to watch the spectacle we're creating in the middle of departures in Los Angeles International. We have attracted the attention of a crowd.

"Let go of my arm, Callum. I swear to God I can make a bigger scene." He tugs my arm, ignoring my threat, and hauls me along behind him. When the initial flash blinds me, we run for the VIP lounge. He pushes the door open and yanks me in. We both lean against it, out of breath. He turns, placing one hand against the wall above my head and the other gripping my hip. I've never had to run away from the press before, and my heart is racing. My anger flares as I stare into those blue pools. "You're such a fucking asshole, Callum Hayes."

"Baby, please just let me explain?"

"What? That you want both of us because that's what the bad-boy rock star does?"

"No! Fuck, Tayla. Would you listen?" Before he can explain, someone pushes on the door, slamming me into Callum.

"What are you two doing? Actually, I don't need to know." Kierra peers at us and the blush on my cheeks heat my face.

"Nothing. Callum was about to justify why he's fucking his ex again." Dismay is evident in her expression. I assume he didn't mention it to her either.

"I'm not screwing her. We were photographed by her paparazzi friends who saw her walking into me when I was getting you dinner." His stare is heated and sears my skin. I recall he went out a few weeks ago to order takeaway from my favorite Chinese restaurant.

"Oh."

"Do I get a make-up kiss now?" He leans in, and I hear the groan behind me from Liam when he pipes up.

"No. We don't need your public displays of

149

affection, making us queasy before we board the flight."

"Liam, jealousy makes you a grumpy fucker." The brothers spend more time debating who gets more sex than they talk about music. Shaking my head, I take a seat. Callum flops next to me, resting his hand on my thigh. I open my laptop, and I log into the band's social media accounts. The photo is capturing the attention of fans. And already, there are five hundred comments. Many of them are assuming he is back with her, and they're adding a hashtag #GetRidOfArina.

"Cal, have a look at this." I pass him the computer; his expression is not what I'm expecting. The smile that tugs the edge of his mouth is unmistakable.

"It will simmer down. If not, we can respond." Without replying, I shut down my laptop. We're resting in the lounge when I see Ryan and Kierra giggling. They've been close since I first started working here, although I know they're not dating. At least I don't think they are. The boys are secretive. I suppose they have to be. Sneaking a glimpse at Callum, I notice he's jotting phrases in his journal.

"What are you doing?" As I lean in, he jumps, shielding the page from me.

"You're not supposed to see it yet." I narrow my eyes, taking in his expression. He's hiding it, which has me curious. Sometimes his brain doesn't switch off. Constantly creating. "Wait till we've landed, okay?"

"Fine." Sitting back, I cross my arms over my chest and look out the window. The trip is long, but I'm excited to arrive in Europe. Paris is our initial destination. Being with Callum in one of the most romantic cities will be incredible.

The door opens, and two large, uniformed officers join us. Apparently, they're ready for the crew to board the flight. They will escort us to the hangar. With the security detail, it makes moving through the crowd much smoother. Fans are calling out to the band and flashes appear from both sides. Cal is walking next to me; his hand is brushing against me every few seconds.

Once we are onboard, Callum announces our schedule once we land. We have two days before the show, so we'll have time to explore the city. Monday night is the first concert. I'm thrilled to be a part of it. He points out we're welcome to have our dinners in the restaurant with the team or head off on our own.

"That is if you and Tayla can unglue your hips long enough." Liam's remark doesn't go unnoticed, and the annoyance on Callum's face is obvious. The air is heavy with frustration between them, and I wonder if something happened.

"Liam, I would appreciate respect for my girlfriend." A huff from his brother and Callum continues talking. We're staying in Paris until Tuesday morning, and then we're off to Germany, Holland, Russia, and lastly, London. The finale in the UK has been extensively advertised, and I realize that playing Wembley will be the biggest show in Europe.

Once we reach our cruising altitude, the pilot announces we can undo our safety belts. Stretching my feet out in front of me, I recline my seat and close my eyes. Callum's fingers brush mine. My eyes snap open to find stormy pools of a vivid blue. The salacious expression he's wearing tells me precisely what he has in mind. Leaning in, he whispers in my ear, "Meet me in the back. Two minutes." We're traveling in the band's private jet, and the prospect of joining the mile-high club has my panties soaked and my core pulsing.

My heart thumps against my rib cage. I've done nothing like this before. With a hasty glimpse at the rest of the team, I notice everyone is watching a movie or are busy with their phones. I shift out of my seat and make my way to the rear of the plane.

A door opens, and Callum grasps my wrist, yanking me into the restroom. Even though it's larger than one on a normal airline, it's still cramped with his enormous frame taking up most of the space. With a palm over my mouth, my body quivers with anticipation. "Shh . . . You need to be quiet." I nod. He lowers his hand and twirls me around.

"What are you doing? There are people a few feet away," I hiss at him.

The grin and naughty glint in his eyes say he

doesn't care where we were. "I missed touching you." When he reaches out to tuck a stray strand of hair behind my ear, I withdraw from his touch. The rumors about Callum and Liam flirting with fans and groupies have me on edge. My chest tightens at the prospect of having to share him. I realize it comes with the job, but deep down, I find it challenging to see.

"You want me before we land in Paris?" The flicker of recognition in his eyes doesn't go unnoticed; the meaning in my statement is obvious. His life is an open book. To me. To the world. The only thing he has kept secret is me. We ultimately decided it was best, but now I wonder if it was.

He grips my shoulders roughly, the frustration marring his perfectly handsome face. Those sky-blue pools turn dark and stormy. "Tayla, I'm yours. How would you like me to prove that to you?" My mouth opens and closes. Words fail me. I'm too distracted by his hard body pressed against me to start this fight.

"Callum, forget it." My palms flat against his chest, I push, but he doesn't relent. He's stronger than me, and I don't stand a chance of getting him away from me.

His eyes sear into mine. "No, I will not. For God's sake woman, I want you. How can you not see that?" His voice grows louder than we both expect. I peer at him, not finding an explanation to my uncertainty. I know it's my insecurity, not being good enough to be dating a famous rock star. Someone who could have any girl in the world, yet he's standing locked in a toilet with me. We both remain silent for a minute, and when nobody knocks on the door to find out what the shouting is about, he hoists me onto the counter.

His lips are on me in an instant. He devours me. Sucking my bottom lip into his hot mouth. His teeth sink in, biting, causing me to moan. Our tongues fight for control. I let him have it. I taunt him by sucking on his tongue, flicking my own over his. The groan I love rumbles deep in his throat. My concerns about groupies forgotten because at that point all that matters is him and me.

His body is flush against mine, and I feel his thick cock pressing against my core. I wore a skirt, and I'm so glad I did. "Callum . . ." I moan into the kiss.

He ignores me and nips at my neck. His teeth graze the soft, sensitive flesh, sucking it into his mouth. The sound of his zipper is music to my ears. He shuffles his jeans and briefs to his knees. Then I hear the familiar foil ripping, and his hands are on my thighs, splaying me before him. He nudges my thong to the side, and his index finger dips into my molten core, slipping through my drenched folds. Those beautiful fingers that can strum any guitar string to perfection are now strumming my clit, making music with my body.

Those expert digits are replaced with his

hard shaft. With a torturous, slow movement, he thrusts into me. As soon as he's fully seated, he stops. My legs wrap around his waist, and my arms hold on to his neck. Dark blue bores into brown pools. The emotion in them is evident. Something I never considered I would have. It's scary. *Love.* He didn't say it, but he didn't need to. I see it.

Our bodies move simultaneously, perfectly in sync. My head drops as he draws out till only the crown is inside me. With sudden ferocity, he slams back into me. So deep, every nerve in my body comes alive with pleasure. He reaches between us and teases and tortures my hardened bud with the pad of his thumb. The intense orgasm that tightens in my abdomen splinters through me. I squeeze my eyes so tight stars burst behind my eyelids. My mouth latches on his shoulder, and my teeth sink in, biting to keep from screaming out loud.

My pussy pulses around him, and his body tenses. His cock thickens and jerks. With a rough growl, his orgasm shudders through him. "God, you will be the fucking death of me, woman," he hisses into my hair as he calms. I cling to him for a moment, not wanting to see the love in his gaze. It disarms me, and I need to stay strong. Love is something I can't accept. Not now. If he says it, and I find him with another girl, I would be destroyed.

He lifts me off him and lets my legs down. "Will you please believe I want you?" His plea is thick with emotion, and I can't find my voice. I nod and smile.

When we take our seats, I realize nobody even noticed we left. I pull my Kindle from my bag and open my latest novel. Callum's hand on my thigh is warm and welcome. The memory of him filling me moments before makes the butterflies in my stomach flutter.

Glancing over at him, I mouth *Not here*. He leans in, and his hot breath on my neck sends a tingle to my core.

"I love keeping you distracted." With a slow and deliberate movement, he traces his tongue along the shell of my ear, sending another jolt of pleasure over my body.

"Stop it," I hiss at him, and he laughs. Liam glares over at us.

"Guys, get a room!" I turn to him, watching his glare travel down to my thighs. I don't realize why until I follow his gaze. Callum's hand pushed my skirt up a little higher than it should have. Tugging it back down, I straighten in the seat.

"Aren't you meant to be working, Liam?" My reply is terse, making him smile slowly. There's something dark in his eyes. He doesn't trust me. Cal told me he voiced his concern about me selling my story to the press. That's what Callum's ex did. She ran straight to the papers when things went south between them. Somehow, I want to assure him I'm not a fame whore. No way do I need it or want it. I hate people who use others, and if it takes all my life to prove that to Liam, I will. I'm falling for Callum; there's no doubt about that. He accepts me for who I am. My feelings for him are the most real I have ever known. The connection we have is intense. If that turns to love, then I need to curb my insecurities and make it work.

As we pull up to the Terrass hotel in black SUVs with blackened windows, I notice there aren't many photographers around — yet. We didn't have time to update our social media to let everyone know we had arrived. It was easier to travel from the airport to the hotel without being pursued. The reception is quiet, and when we get to the desk, a polished receptionist glances up with a perfect smile.

"*Bonne après-midi*, Mr. Hayes. *Bienvenue.*" *Good afternoon, Mr. Hayes. Welcome.*

"*En anglais, s'il vous plaît?*" *Can you speak English, please?* She nod.

"My apologies, Monsieur. Let me check you in. I will have the luggage sent up to the individual suites." Her accent is perfectly French, but her English impeccable. She hands out the keys to the crew, and we say our goodbyes, agreeing to dinner downstairs at eight that evening.

Callum and I make our way up to our room. He opens the door and allows me to step inside first. I gasp. This isn't your average room; it's the penthouse suite. Spacious. Luxurious. Exquisite. The contemporary furniture is a contrast to the impressive view of the city from the floor-to-ceiling patio doors. It has an open-plan living room complete with sofa, coffee table, and desk. In the opposite corner is a miniature bar fridge and two wingback chairs. The terrace has a table with two chairs that overlook the rooftops of Paris below, including the *Sacre Coeur* and the famous Eiffel Tower.

I wander into the bathroom, which has black tiles along the walls, and an enormous shower and separate bath. A Jacuzzi overlooking the rooftops and a private sauna call my name. The bedroom, sheer luxury, features a king-sized bed sitting in the center of the room against one wall with a private outer area. Everything screams decadence. It isn't over the top but understated opulence that is not lost on me.

"Callum, this is crazy. We're only here for three days." When I turned to face him, his expression is filled with excitement. He shrugs casually.

"Only the best." He winks and grabs his laptop. "I need to finish work before dinner."

"Okay, I'll have a shower. I stink." He chortles. Leaning in, he sniffs me and peers into my eyes.

"You're right. You smell delicious." Poking my tongue out at him, I tug off my shoes and pad into the bathroom. Turning on the taps, letting it heat, I shed my clothes. As I step into the warm spray, it massages my aching muscles. I shampoo my hair with the lavender-scented bottle they supplied.

Stepping out onto the plush rug, I grasp the fluffy towel and dry myself. The complimentary robes are soft and warm. I pull one on and make my way to the bedroom. Callum is standing in the doorway of the terrace, dressed in a pair of sweats with a bare torso. He's deep in thought and doesn't hear me behind him. I take a moment to watch him. Drinking him in hungrily, enjoying the view of my man.

"You can stop gawking at me now," he states in an amused tone, startling me from my blatant staring. I step farther into the room. There's music playing on his laptop from the bed. I recognize the song that just started, "Monster" by Aaron Richards.

"Don't flatter yourself, Hayes. I had an amazing shower." He twists and grins.

"Take off the robe." The rough, demanding timbre of his voice sends a tingle down my spine. I loosen the sash and slip the robe over my shoulders. My hair is knotted in a loose bun, the tips still soaked, dripping onto my back. His hungry gaze roams from my face to my neck and over my breasts. The trail of his eyes leaves a fire in their wake.

When his gaze reaches my bare pussy, my body trembles in response. "I love looking at you, trembling for me." The deep rasp in his voice is thick with lust. "Come here, Petal." The three steps it takes to position myself in front of him are easy. When I stand flush with him, I raise my eyes to find his in a fierce stare. His left hand comes up and lightly trails fingertips from my exposed neck to my shoulder. Another tremble courses through me. Goosebumps rise over my skin. A low moan escapes my parted lips. I reach for him, but his expression stops me. "Did I tell you to touch me?" The naughty smirk that pulls the corner of his mouth causes me to smile. I shake my head.

His hand drifts back up, and he clutches my hair in a tight grip, holding me steady at an angle. His mouth slants over mine as our lips crash together. He licks the seam of my mouth, and I reward him the access he demands.

The kiss becomes hungry, eager. Deep. Sensual. When he breaks the kiss, my lips feel cold without him. He still has a steady grip on me, and I can't move. His teeth graze over the sensitive spot behind my ear, earning him a whimper. The action so erotic.

Slow.

Soft.

Agonizing.

Torturous.

My body comes alive under his touch, and I can't think about anything else. Every nerve sparks when his teeth graze my hardened nipples. He laves and teases them until they tighten. When he bites on one, he tweaks and tugs the other with this thumb and forefinger.

The painful pleasure sends jolts directly to my throbbing clit.

This man knows my body better than I do; he has my senses on high alert. I quiver, my pussy pulsing. I need him more than my next breath. Everything past and present doesn't matter but this moment. He licks a warm wet trail from my shoulder to my ear, then lightly blows on the path left by his tongue. The hair on the back of my neck stands on end. "Callum, please? I can't take it anymore."

"You are mine. Do you hear me? Do not question me again." He pauses and stares at me. Making sure I heard each word he said. I nod. My voice evades me. This isn't the time to be talking about it. I ache for him. He pulls me over to the terrace. The Eiffel Tower winks at us in the dusk sky. The lights of the city shine below. "Hold on tight, Petal, because I am painfully hard, and you are going to feel me so deep inside you there won't be any doubt who you belong to. I will claim your mind, body, and soul. And when I am finished, your heart will be mine too." He kicks my feet apart as I clutch the rail of the balcony in front of me. He has me, every part of me. Only I'm too afraid to tell him.

I shiver when his hot breath hits my core. I'm dripping with arousal for him. At this point, any touch will send me spiraling. His fingers caress my inner thighs, teasing the delicate skin. My knees wobble, and my grip tightens, turning my knuckles white. His tongue flicks out and laps at my sopping pussy, skimming along the slick folds.

"Fuck, you taste perfect, Petal. Like the sweet nectar of the gods. But you're only wet for this god to enjoy, aren't you, baby?" His voice is so raspy I almost come undone.

"Yesss." My voice is a low hiss. He rises, and I hear him shuffle out of his sweats. They drop to the floor, and the foil tearing sends a shiver through me. I peer behind me and watch him grip his thick, hard cock, teasing me with the tip. I push back against him. Needing him inside me. Now.

"Do you enjoy making me crazy, Tayla?" he asks hoarsely, his voice full of desire. I nod. He rains a slap on my ass. Hard. "I asked you a question." My voice evades me.

"I . . ." My mumble doesn't suffice, and I feel a second sharp sting. I'm aching and dripping wet from the spanking he's giving me. "Yes . . . Yes, Callum," I mumble, my skin tingling, but I have never been so turned on in my whole life.

"Then you need to be punished, Petal," he growls as he plunges into me. So deep, as he promised. My body completely filled. I scream his name as he invades my heated tunnel.

"Callum!" He starts with slow thrusts, allowing me to adjust to him. His hands grip my hips as he drives into me. I'm far beyond thinking clearly, my moans and mewls surrounding us in the darkness. Another loud smack echoes in the night. He tugs and unties my hair. When it falls down my back, he fists it and tugs.

He leans forward and hisses in my ear, "Mine. Do you understand?" I try nodding, but he has me in a vice-like hold — my orgasm building. Tightening my stomach and my pussy cinching around him. I'm teetering on the edge, needy for release. He pulls out abruptly, and I whimper at the loss. Spinning me to face him, he lifts me. Instinctively, I wrap my legs around his waist and hold on to his neck. His lust-filled eyes meet mine.

"Hold on to me, baby," he growls and plunges into me again, walking us to the far end of the terrace. The tiles flush against my back as he pins me between his body and the icy wall. Without warning, he repeatedly thrusts into my heated pussy, fucking me. It's rough, deep, hard, and I don't want it any other way. The fire in my belly licks its way through my veins. My blood heated with passion as it courses through me. My nails dig into his shoulders, and he groans in response.

He leans into my neck. "I crave you so fucking much. This tight pussy is made to take my cock. Only mine. No other man will make you feel like this. Ever." His words are my undoing. My release splinters through me, and I cry out — screaming his name repeatedly.

A chant.

A chorus.

A prayer.

He continually drives into me. Once, twice,

and with the third, he stiffens — his cock pulses inside me. With a throaty growl of my name, he unravels. His teeth sink into my shoulder. The pain sends a jolt to my throbbing clit, and another wave of pleasure washes over me.

"Fuck." Callum's tone is low as he hisses the word in my ear. Yes. *Fuck.* He slips out of me gently. "Guess it's time for dinner." Our eyes meet and I snicker as he lets me down gradually. A gentle kiss, and we pad into the bedroom to get dressed.

"At least Paris knows Callum Hayes is here."

"You're fucking loud. It's seductive and sexy, Petal. I love it when you scream my name." He winks at me as he pulls his jeans on. Shaking my head, I find the dress I planned to wear tonight. This will be an interesting tour.

CALLUM

The venue is filling up with the VIP ticket holders. I look around for Tayla, but she isn't in the crew area. We had the most amazing night, but this morning she seemed distant. Like she was trying to push me away. There is love in her eyes when she looks at me, and that's what scared her. I want to talk to her, but we've been so busy today. When the time is right, she needs to move past the pain. I wish I could take it away. I want to fuck it out of her if I could. It would be my pleasure. And hers. Ultimately, it has to be her choice to let me in.

"Bro. Did you finish the set list? I need to run through it in my head." I face my brother. Liam doesn't trust my relationship with Tay because of my history with Arina, but he needs to get over it. Tayla isn't out to fuck me over. She has her own demons she struggles with.

"Yeah, these are the thirteen songs I chose. Those three are acoustic, so you'll have a break halfway through the set. Give a copy to Ryan." He nods and turns to leave. Before he walks away, he cuts a glance back to me. "I'm sorry if I have been harsh with her. You're my baby brother. I don't want to see you hurt." Our eyes meet, and I acknowledge him with a nod.

He's only a year older, but he likes to think there's more of a gap between us. Emotionally, there is. He doesn't let anyone in. Ever. Whereas I do. Well, I did once, and now with Tayla. She's woven her way into my life.

"Callum!" I peer down at the group of scantily clad women in their early twenties — a guess — that are vying for my attention by waving at me. I give a smirk and wink. Their squeals rise in decibels. When I whirl around, I find Tay glaring at me. I realize she's apprehensive about me being on tour with fans and groupies, but she doesn't have to worry. She's the only one who can make me rock hard with a smile. Tayla Quinn has been written into my heart, my mind, and into the depths of my soul.

"You're the center of attention as always, Hayes." Her voice is strained with anger. Since we're keeping our relationship private, I can't pull her into my arms. I would love to announce my feelings for her. And I plan to do it. On her birthday. It's my gift to her.

"Is this what it will be like? I can't help it, Petal." My response isn't what she wants to hear, because I stride towards her, and she takes two steps backward. Pain constricts my chest. "Jesus, baby, we chose to keep you off the radar for this tour." She spins on her heel and races off, leaving me staring at her departing form.

"She's a tough cookie, Cal. You need to talk to her. Go. I can deal with the crowd. Just be here for sound check, or they will cause a scene." My best friend — besides Liam — Ryan is like a brother.

"I know, but she preferred no one to find out about us. Now every time a girl glances at me, she freaks." Shaking my head, I place my guitar on the platform.

"Yeah, I get that. But you have to understand, it's painful to see the man you're in love with flirting with other girls." My eyes snap in his direction. *Love? Did she love me?*

"What?"

"She's in love with you, man. Anyone can see it. If you can't, then you're blind." His words sink deep into the recesses of my mind. My heart knew the moment I looked at her; she was the one. Could I give her what she needs? Is there a chance she will accept my very public life? "Go to her."

Leaving my best friend, I run after the woman I love. As I pass the crew, I ask the other sound engineer where she went. He points to the dressing rooms. I make my way to the catering room, where I hear voices coming from. It's Liam and Tayla. Pushing the door open, I find his arms wrapped around her. My fucking girl. "What the fuck is going on?" Rage burns in my veins.

They both jump apart. Her eyes are void of guilt. "I apologized to Tayla. I was being a douche, and I told her to invite her sister to the London show." Two strides and I am next to her.

"Fine. Leave us. I need to talk to her." My words hold a threat to him. With a shrug, he walks out. When I hear the click, I turn to her and cup her face in my hands. "Why were you in my brother's arms?"

"He gave me a hug, Callum. It was nothing." She stares at me. A smile on her lips makes me calm down. "Are you jealous, Hayes?" Her calling me by my last name is an indication of her wanting to rile me up. This time, though, she won't get it right.

"Come here, baby." I pull her into an embrace. "So, my brother and your sister, huh? Are you trying to matchmake them?" She nods with a small giggle. "How do you know he will like her?"

"Because I showed him a photo of her on my phone. That's when he said that she has to be one of his VIP guests." I laugh so loud the sound echoes through the empty room. Trust my fucking brother. He can be such a horny fucker. Each of us gets five VIP tickets for friends or family. Liam usually invites numerous models as guests, and they never decline.

The whole evening, I have my gaze latched on Tayla. I perform for the crowd, but she is the center of my mind. Standing on the side of the stage with Kierra, I sneak glances at her constantly. The fans are incredible as usual. Singing along and jumping around to the more hardcore songs. When I sing "Damaged Angel", my eyes lock on the girl standing in the shadows. Nobody knows though. I set up the guitar and microphone, so it looks like I'm singing to the camera recording the show. But this is for her. Always.

The tour went smoothly. Tay and I found a rhythm. I wanted to tell her I love her, but I waited. The time wasn't right, and tonight will be the biggest test of all. I'm backstage getting ready. The girls are in the Meet and Greet, setting up for the fans to have their photos taken with us. I have a bad feeling tonight. No reason, but something doesn't sit right in my gut. I know Arina and a few of her friends from the modeling agency arrived an hour ago. They had VIP tickets, and I should have told Tay, but not wanting to upset her, I kept it quiet. Now, here I am with a pounding heart. I realize she'll find out.

I'm so fucking terrified of her breaking things off that I just acted like it's any other show. Why? Because I am a dick. When my dressing room door opens, I don't turn to see who it is.

I should have.

"Petal, did you come to give me a good luck kiss?" I chuckle, but as I spin around, I am greeted with those emerald eyes I once loved getting lost in. "What the fuck are you doing here?"

"I came to see the famous Callum Hayes. My first love." Her voice and accent are ice water rushing through my veins. *How was I ever in love with this woman?* She's taller than Tayla by a few inches. She has short, dark brown hair, and her face is all angles and a fake pout that must be the result of too much Botox, whereas my girl is natural, pristine, and innocent. Beautiful in a way that can make any grown man drop to his knees. Which I always do.

"What do you want? We are not together anymore. I don't want you here. How many times do I have to reject you?" When she steps forward, I wince. She notices my reaction. There is no mistaking that I don't feel anything for her. The distaste in my statement undeniable, but she never did take no for an answer.

She slips the flimsy straps of her dress over her shoulders. The skinny dark-haired girl is now standing in front of me in nothing but a tiny black thong. Her hands grasp my biceps, holding me like a lifeline. The problem is, I cut that line a long time ago. She leans up and plants a kiss on my cheek. "I miss you, Callum." My name on her lips makes me sick. I grip her arms to push her away as her mouth moves to mine. When the door swings open for a second time, and I turn my gaze, which locks onto brown eyes and blonde hair. Pain etched on the face of the girl I love but am too much of a pussy to tell her those three words. *Fuck!* I shove Arina off me and bolt after Tayla, who runs like she's being chased by her demons.

"Tayla! Petal!" I call out to her. This time she doesn't stop. There's no way to make her listen to me. I am such a fucking idiot. I should have told that bitch to leave me alone when she strolled into my room. "Tay, for god's sake! Stop!" We reach the end of the hallway, and she's trapped between me and the fire escape. Pulling at the exit, it opens suddenly, and she runs outside.

"Just go, Callum. I can't look at you right now."

"No! She came into the room. I told her I don't want her." I take a tentative step toward her, and she steps back. This is getting me nowhere.

"Fuck you, Hayes! Okay, fuck you, because it sure didn't look like it. You need to be on stage in ten minutes." Her eyes are brimming with tears, but being Tayla, she doesn't want me to see her cry. She turns and looks out at the dark parking lot. Pain sears through me. My chest is tight with emotion. I hurt her. If I had been honest, this wouldn't have happened.

"Fuck the stage! Listen. Hear me. Please?" Her glare holds venom that poisons my veins, and I realize she won't open up and let me in. I need to let her calm down. This isn't over. "This isn't over," I repeat the words, spin on my heel, and make my way into the venue.

The show is perfect except for one thing; Tayla hates me. She doesn't even look at me. The crew are in the catering tent as the champagne flows, and everyone seems relaxed. Tay sits with Ki and Ryan which those two have grown closer by the day. I am thrilled for him since he deserves to find happiness.

"So Arina screwed up again." Liam's voice behind me has me turning to deal with my brother. "Hey, man, chill. I was just asking. I told you that little slut was trouble from the first time she walked into our dressing room."

"Why? Because she wouldn't fuck you?" It's a low blow, but I'm angry. He's right. There were warning signs about her since I laid eyes on her. I'm such a self-absorbed dick. Dating a model appealed to me. The fake tits and smile didn't faze me. It was more than a year ago, and I was having fun. At least I thought I was. Now when my gaze settles on the blonde beauty who is shooting daggers at me, I can't help thinking what a fucking idiot I am.

I have to make this right. Somehow. Walking over to where they sit, I play it cool. "You guys ready for London?" Ryan turns and fist pumps me.

"Man, you do not understand. I need to go to a pub and get myself a decent beer."

"You mean that warm shit they pass off as

beer?" I laugh.

"It's excellent stuff man. Seriously." I nod. My gaze wanders over Ki and onto the reason I am standing here rambling about stupid crap.

"Tay, you looking forward to your birthday, darling?" Brown eyes glare at me. Her face is stone. No emotion. Only a vacant stare.

"Well, Ryan. I need another drink." Kierra, ever the subtle one in the group, yanks him to his feet, and Tayla and I are left alone.

"Was the show okay?" I question her tentatively.

"Yeah." She angles her head and glances over at the team playing beer pong. Someone misses, and they have to chug their drink. A smile hints on her lips, and my heart flips. Jesus, I'm a pussy for this girl.

"London will be fun." Her glare shoots to me, and she narrows those beautiful chestnut eyes on me.

"Callum, don't. This whole situation was a mistake. I'm not into sharing the person I—" She stops mid-sentence and rises from the sofa. "Just leave it. I am fine." She is so strong and weak at the same time. Her heart is breaking. I can hear it in her words. I realize she won't let up, but I will not stop pushing. She's mine. I will make this right.

We land in London three days after the

show in Russia. Every moment with Tayla is like talking to a brick wall. She's professional when she speaks to me, but the warmth is gone. It's in those empty nights I realize without a doubt I fucking love her. There's only one thing I can do. I know if I'm going to win this girl back, I'm going to have to put my heart on my sleeve.

Walking into the Arch Hotel in the center of London, I make my way to the welcome desk. The receptionist checks us in, but when Tayla walks off with Kierra, I can't take it anymore. This is ridiculous. "Tayla, we need to talk. It's been three days." She gives me a small nod. I glance at Kierra, and she walks off, pinning me with a glare of warning.

"I don't think there's much we can talk about."

"Come with me." I pull her into the waiting elevator and hit the floor for our rooms. I calm when she doesn't refuse or fight me. "I just want to talk." We step out of the elevator, and I unlock my room, allowing her to step inside first. Her gaze is uncertain for a few minutes, and when I don't move, she steps inside. I follow her and close the door.

"Talk. You have five minutes."

"Look, Petal. You walked in at the wrong time. I was telling her she needed to leave. I told her I do not love her or want her. She grabbed me and leaned up when you saw us."

"Callum, I get you explaining what happened. Right now, I think it's safer if we keep our distance. I'm sorry. I don't want to hurt anymore." She drops her gaze as she passes me; her sweet scent assaulting me. She reaches the door and stops, her hand on the doorknob. Before she opens it, she cuts a quick glance at me. That beautiful smile I love curled on her lips. Only, it isn't her happy one; it's painfully sad. "Goodbye, Callum." With that, she leaves my room. Cold and empty. I sink onto the sofa, my head whirling with what this means. She said the words that sliced through me. It's done. Final. So deathly final.

The click rung in my ears like an alarm. When Tayla walked out, my heart and my soul went with her. With sudden ferocity, words pound in my mind. I snatch my notebook and pen and write. There is only one thing I can do. To make her see. There is no fucking way she's leaving me. Not now. Never.

TAYLA

The click of the door shatters me. My throat tightens painfully. The tears that threaten burn my eyes. I bolt to Kierra's room and pound on the door. When it swings open, I peer at her blurry form. Her face filled with concern, and that's when I break down. She draws me inside, and I crumple to the floor. The anguish in my chest is unlike anything I've ever felt. Even when he hurt me. That was nothing compared to having your heart crushed, your soul destroyed, and your life crumble in front of you.

"What happened? Do I need to kick his ass?" I shake my head. The sobs that escape me are inhuman. I can't breathe. A hole inside has left me vacant. Kierra lifts me and sits me on the sofa. I crave to curl up and hide. For days. Weeks. Years.

"I can't . . . It feels like . . . I can't . . ." I choke in between wails. "Breathe . . . It's . . . Hurts . . ." I ramble in between choking gasps. Her arms wrap around me, trying to shield me from something, but it doesn't work. There isn't anything that could stop this agony.

"Shh, come on, honey. He's a guy. He may have fucked up, but he loves you." Her words slowly settle into my fuzzy brain, and I bolt up. Through my teary gaze, I gawk at her as if she has two heads. Then suddenly, I snicker. *Love? Is she joking?*

"He doesn't love me. Callum is a famous rock star. He has girls falling over themselves to be his."

"Yes, that's true. But I know him, Tayla, and the only girl whose presence he chooses to be in is yours. Trust me when I say this. I have seen him with girls, loads of them for years. He has never looked at anyone the way he looks at you."

I sit silent, my fingers twirling the tissue in my hands. My tears stopped, and I sigh heavily. "Do you think I should give him a second chance?" When I peer at Kierra, she shrugs.

"It's not my call, honey. How do you feel? I wouldn't trust that little bitch as far as I could throw her. Cal hates her, so I know that nothing happened. You also need to think about something else. If you can't take seeing him interact with the fans, if you can't handle the spotlight, then walk away now. But if you love him and you're prepared to fight for him, then do it. God knows I have lost someone because of fear. Don't let that happen to you." She gets up and heads to her suitcase, still in the living room. "I will leave you and go change. If you want to stay here tonight, you can. Remember, he will not give up on you. He's a stubborn asshole, but he's also filled with love. He wants to give it to someone. And that someone is you." With a modest smile, she turns and shuffles into the bedroom. The door closes with a simple click, leaving me to my thoughts. When she emerges fifteen minutes later, all dressed up; she glances at me.

"You coming to dinner, darling?"

"I think it's better if I stay here. There's a lot I need to figure out." With a nod, I'm alone.

I turn the TV on, but I'm not watching it. There's one person I know will listen to me grumble. Pulling out my phone, I call Emma.

"Sis. How are you, babe?"

"Okay. I suppose."

"What happened? You sound like shit." I chuckle, and it hurts. I shouldn't laugh when my heart is broken.

"I broke up with Callum. Now I am second-guessing myself."

"What? Why? Did he fucking hurt you?" My sister is adorable when she freaks out. Not much can appease her.

"No, his ex was in his dressing room the night of the gig in Russia, and I caught them."

"Did the fucker cheat on you? I will cut his dick off." Her tone is laden with rage.

"He didn't. Nothing physically happened."

"Then why did you break up?" That's the question I have been asking myself since Ki left.

"I don't know."

"Maybe you need time. Visit Lee tomorrow. He was asking for you."

"Yes, I guess I will. Thanks, darling. See you at the show."

"I can't wait. And tell Liam he's in for a night of debauchery."

"Oh, God." My groan is loud. "That is a visual I do not want. Thank you, baby sister." Her giggle is contagious, and I grin.

"Don't be such a prude. I reckon Callum is a tiger in bed."

"Goodbye, Emma." Another chuckle from her, and we finally hang up. My heart feels lighter. Tomorrow, I will talk to Cal. I need him. We can work this out. I couldn't look at him right now. Not yet. I have to consider what Kierra and my sister suggested.

There was something about the way Ki was convinced he loves me that forces me to believe her. He has never mentioned he loves me. I suppose we didn't have time to talk about our relationship during the tour. There was constantly other shit going on that I didn't consider a future with anyone.

Did I love him enough to get past my own insecurities? He's proved that he cares for me, but love? The film onscreen ends, and I realize I need to sleep. The concert is tomorrow, and Em is right; I should visit Lee. One of my best friends. He's been in the Army for years. I met him when I was on a two-month holiday. My eyes are puffy from sobbing. I stand and pad to the bathroom.

I splash my face with lukewarm water, then I brush my teeth and clamber into bed. I have a long day ahead — my birthday and the show. I decide I'll fight for my man, and that requires a decent night's rest.

I wake with a start as my alarm buzzes next to me. I shut it off, roll over, and open my eyes. The sun hasn't even risen yet, and I groan. This is way too fucking early. Swinging my feet over the edge of the bed, I stand and head to my suitcase and grab my workout clothes.

Padding to the bathroom, I get changed. I want to get a run in before I have to be at the venue. The fresh air always helps clear my head. I have to decide how I'll broach the subject with Callum.

As scared as I am, I have to give us a chance.

Last night I told him goodbye, but if he knows me, he'll know I didn't mean it. I dress in my running gear and quietly leave Kierra's room. Once I'm in the elevator, I plug in my earbuds and turn on an upbeat playlist.

The first song is "Damaged Angel". I'm excited to hear the new songs the boys are working on. There have been a few times I saw lyrics on Callum's notebook. I wish he would share them with me.

Out on the road, I run up Great Cumberland

Place, toward Hyde Park.

My legs carry me to the building I haven't been to in such a long time. To a friend I miss more than I realized. Two and a half miles, and I make it in the shortest time ever. When I reach the massive building near St James Tube Station, I get to the gate, finding a few soldiers milling around. My feet bring me to the Wellington Barracks. Suddenly, I'm unsure why I came here.

"Kin ah help ye, lassie?" Can I help you, miss?

His accent is thick Scots. Probably from mid-Scotland, just outside Edinburgh is my first guess.

"Aye, dae ye ken, Lee?" Yes, do you know, Lee?

I haven't spoken Scottish slang in just over a year, and I'm surprised it comes easily. His smile is sweet, and he nods.

"Aye. Ah wull ca' him." Yes, I will call him.

I nod and stand to the side as the enormous, looming gates open. One of the army trucks pulls out and drives off. I take a few deep breaths and think about seeing my best friend again. I spent a lot of time in London since my family moved here. My father transferred here through the company he landed a job with after the terrible incident with his partner.

They dealt with high-end insurance for international corporations. When they branched out to the UK and offered my dad a job, he agreed. After losing everything, he needed to do something for him and my mom. His parents grew up in England, and for him to be here was like coming home. My parents own a house not far from here. I made friends with most of the locals that frequented the pub that Em and I visit. That's when I met Lee. He's the sweetest boy I know. We were close until he got a girl pregnant and she decided that him having a female friend wasn't appropriate.

I reach down and wrap my arms around my knees, stretching my hamstrings, when I hear a familiar voice. *"Thare is a fucking bonny sight."* There is a fucking beautiful sight.

I straighten and come face to face with sparkling green eyes. The naughty smirk on his face is so familiar I almost burst into tears. If it wasn't for him, I'm not sure I would have gotten through what happened to me. I run up to him, throwing my arms around his neck, nuzzling my face in his clean, soapy scent — my best friend.

"Ye a'richt bonny?" You all right, beautiful?

I nod into his jacket and giggle when he spins me around.

"Can you cut the Scottish now?" He flashes me a smile, and his eyes crease.

"Aye, darlin'. Do you wanna grab a coffee?"

"Please. I just popped by to see how you're doing with fatherhood." I glance at him, and his jaw tightens.

"Not good. She's taken off home. *Didnae* like London. Back in bonny Scotland." My heart hurts for him. His girlfriend can be a tyrant when she wants to be. "And ye? What ye doin' back?"

"I'm on tour with the band. They're playing Wembley tonight."

"Shite. That's fucking brilliant."

"*Aye*, but I need advice." We walk into Costa coffee, and Lee orders, paying with the notes he pulls from his combat cargo pants. He hands me my cup, and we find a seat.

"Ye askin' me fer advice? Shite, it must be bad." He chuckles, and I swat him.

"I'm in love, Lee. I've fallen, and I don't know what to do. He's wonderful. My insecurities got the better of me, and jealousy seeing him with his ex had me bolting for the nearest door. Nothing happened between them, but I feel so inadequate. I mean, I'm no famous person. Just a woman." Sipping the hot liquid, I peer up at green eyes. He's staring at me with a smirk on his face.

"Ye no more average than any supermodel in a magazine, Tay. You're worthy of someone who can love ye unconditionally. *Dinnae* let him go. If ye love him, *dinnae* walk away." He takes my hand and gives it a squeeze. I feel better about my decision. Last night, I realized running away is what I've been doing all my life. If Callum chooses me, then I'll give us a chance.

"Thank you, soldier." I mock salute him, which cause him to chuckle. We sit for a few more minutes. Lee gives me the rundown on what is happening with the Army. He wants to leave soon. Another year, and he'll be out. We rise and step out of the shop. Back on the sidewalk, we head toward the barracks.

"C'moan, darlin', a'm oan guard in an oor. A'm needin' tae git back. 'Twas guid seeing ye. Tak' care ae' yersel'." Come on, darlin', I'm on guard in an hour. I need to get back. It was good seeing you. Take care of yourself.

I shake my head at the thick Scottish he speaks and giggle. He leans in and hugs me. "Bye, soldier. Give the queen a wave from me." When he disappears across the road, I head back to the hotel. With my earbuds in, I weave through people heading to work. It's getting lighter now, and I realize I need to hurry.

When I reach The Arch, I slip into Kierra's room before she wakes. I grab my jeans and tank top, clean underwear, and my toiletries. I walk into the bathroom and turn on the shower. As soon as I step under the spray, my aching muscles relax, calming me. I shut my eyes and think about how I'll approach Callum. *What will I say? Do I tell him I love him?* Honesty is the only way to fix this.

I love and hate being on tour. Running up to the main stage, I notice the crew setting up the microphone and drum kit. How on earth we opened the doors on time, I do not know? We were practically two hours late getting into the venue. One of the team called in sick, so I'm filling in. Once we arrived at Wembley, it all went to hell.

Checking the clipboard Ki gave me, I realize we're just about catching up to our allotted times. I read over the new playlist; it's changed for this show. Maybe this song they've included is from the forthcoming album. Even though I'm supposed to be helping with the keyboard set up, Kierra needs me. So, I have someone stand-in and assist Ryan. Now I'm rushing around like a headless chicken trying to make sure everything is on schedule. We need soundcheck done and dusted, which is essential. The VIP Meet and Greet is in an hour. Then we have a backstage tour. Some lucky girl will be chosen to visit the dressing rooms with Callum himself; this should be interesting. There's always tears and blubbering. I want to chat with him before that, but I can't find him this morning. He isn't answering his phone, and Kierra has no idea where he has disappeared to either.

Being part of a worldwide tour for one of the most famous bands in the world is difficult. Here I am, standing and waiting for the crew to finish, and I'm missing something. As I peer up to the stage, I notice Liam is ready; so is Ryan. The main ingredient is not here — our lead singer. Where the fuck is Cal? He provokes me, and he knows he does it. Being late is what he does best, besides singing, and I suppose looking good in everything he wears. *Tay, get a hold of yourself, You're working!* This is becoming impossible.

There's so much we need to talk about,

and he's MIA. I don't know how we ever get anything done when he arrives late. "Petal . . ." That one word is like oxygen to my lungs. A beat of my heart. And a light in my darkness. We haven't spoken in days. He hasn't called me that in roughly a week. Hearing it at this moment gives me the hope that all is not lost.

I turn to face with the gorgeous sky-blue I've missed. "I wanted to talk to you before soundcheck." With a slow step toward him, I lay a hand on his chest. His breathing hitches and I'm too aware of the heat radiating from him. "I need to try. With you." The grin that cracks on his face is incredible.

"Petal, you're wonderful. I . . . I . . . There's a lot we should discuss, but don't run. Please, just never tell me goodbye again." I nod and smile, placing a chaste kiss on his cheek. He whispers in my ear, "Happy birthday, beautiful." Desire is heavy in the air, and tears threaten. I clear my throat and step back.

"I was about to come find you and kick your ass, but since you've brought me coffee, I will forgive you." He offers me a naughty wink. With a glow of amusement, he shrugs. All the strain has vanished to nothing. My heart overflows with love. Yes, love. For the man who has millions of women begging to be with him. The face girls around the world swoon over. The voice they hang onto. Initially, I wasn't convinced he wasn't a bad boy. He is handsome, has a string of models in his past, and with those cerulean eyes,

I was scared. But it's become difficult to deny my feelings. When he lets that smile loose on me, I'm disarmed. My walls crash and he sees my heart, but more than that, he sees my soul. As much as I push, he pulls. And now, I crave to pull.

"You just love getting your hands on me, baby." His voice is a rough growl in my ear. The shiver that runs over my body has me grinning. He rushes toward the stage and hops up effortlessly. When he faces me again, he calls out, "You can handle me whenever you choose, Petal."

That's what touring with them is like and struggling to get Callum to be professional is a persistent pain in the ass. The band knows we're together, but the fans don't. So, it's been a constant problem to tell him to behave. Putting on my serious face, I call out to him, "In your dreams, Hayes!"

Stormy blue pools sear me. "In yours too, Petal!" he retorts. I shake my head at his overconfident demeanor. His nickname for me has my stomach doing flip-flops. He drops his jacket on the stage, and he grabs the mic with an air of belonging. He was born to be up there.

I never understood it until the first time I saw him perform live. It's true, the band are incredible as a whole, but there is something magnetic about Callum Hayes. And that's why I fell in love with him.

I watch as they fit the microphone stand in place for him. There's electricity in the arena as the guitar chords echo through the emptiness. I can't wait to hear them play Wembley Arena. With sudden ferocity, keyboards and drums come to life and fill the massive, empty venue, pulling me from my thoughts. Seeing Liam in his element is like watching a beast attack its prey. They start with my favorite song, "Damaged Angel."

Were you always there in the darkness?
Watching and waiting for me?
Do you always fight your demons alone?
Let me in, Angel, let me in,

You're broken
Shattered in pieces
And I know you're just a
Damaged Angel

Are you going to let me in?
Will you forgive me?
Now we're both just
Demented souls

You're broken
Shattered in pieces
And I know you're just a
Damaged Angel

Those nights of heat
Take the darkness
Bring me the light
My Damaged Angel

Callum's words echo through the stadium, and goosebumps rise on my skin. The song is haunting with an intense drum solo near the end. When he finishes the last chorus, his eyes meet mine, and the butterflies in my stomach come alive. *I love you. I love you. I love you.* Never did I think he was right for me, but I can't deny my soul its mate. He pins me with a knowing glance. At that moment, there isn't anywhere else I would rather be. I'm at his mercy as he holds more than just my body. He holds something I kept hidden for far too long — my heart.

CALLUM

As soon as I step onto the stage, I rule. This is my territory; everybody recognizes that. Since I started performing roughly a decade ago, my life transformed. I needed to leave the small town where I was born to come into my own. The first few years of my fame took its toll. I did some foolish things. I screwed up big time. When I was with Arina, I fell down a sordid dark hole. I look back and wonder what the fuck I was thinking. Tayla has changed me. I have something to live for. In her, I found a connection. A deep and meaningful purpose. If only she would quit being so fucking stubborn.

When I finish the song, my gaze darts up. She's there. The angel who's walked into my life. The girl with the chestnut eyes. Tayla is a challenge, and I fucking love it. When we met, I told her I would change her mind. She didn't believe me. Now, the blush that spreads on her cheeks every time I sing the lyrics to her is unmistakable.

In the months we've spent together, Tay's

pushed me away more times than I care to remember. Her stubbornness makes me want her more. Her past is filled with anguish, with what that monster did to her. I would love to get my hands on him. How I wish I could. There are moments I see the pain in her eyes, and I want to take it away. I have seen her scars. They make her the woman I love. I know why she loves "Damaged Angel." That's what she is — my beautiful, damaged angel.

I have spent days trying to prove to her she can trust me; if only she would open up to me. The first day I saw her, I realized I wanted her. I'm persuasive, but she is definitely not a pushover, and that made me crave her more. Like I said, I love a challenge, and this right here is why I am staring straight at her as I finish the lyrics of our single "Damaged Angel." I turn to my brother; he's wearing his shit-eating grin. As usual, he's dressed in a cutout tank top. No doubt to show off to the thousands of girls when we do the Meet and Greet later.

"Callum, that sounded great. Are you going to do another song?" Her voice is a fucking melody I want on repeat. The long, sleek, blonde hair that hangs down the middle of her back shines under the low lighting. It gives her an ethereal glow. Her face, though, is far from angelic. Her heated bitchy stare sends a jolt to my crotch. She's fucking sexy when she's angry.

"Do we have time, Petal?" Her nickname will make her smile. The expression she offers is priceless. Liam is chuckling behind me. If only he knew how many times this girl has brought me to my knees, literally and figuratively.

She looks at the clipboard she's holding. I know she has the playlist for the show. She'll see the new song I added this morning. "You have twenty minutes before we do the M&G." She glances up. My gaze falls on her mouth, then travels south. Dressed in a cutout T-shirt, the collar is low, and her cleavage is peeking out. *Did I mention I love being on stage?* From up here, I can see exactly what I crave. Supple, silky, and sweet. Tayla Quinn.

"One more. Any requests, gorgeous?" My stare burns into her, and her skin turns a subtle shade of pink. That is the view I have been living for, for months since I met this feisty woman.

"Um . . . Well, since you've asked me. Why don't you do this . . . 'Between Love & Fire'?" The confusion on her face has her brows creasing. Perfect. She wants the song I wrote for her. *Good.*

"You sure?" The grin on my face must give me away because the challenge in her scowl is adorable. *Fine, you want it, Petal? You got it.*

"Drums." I nod, and Liam picks up his cue. As the keyboard comes in, I latch my eyes on her, and I sing the words that came to me last night when she said goodbye.

You walked out the door,
The emptiness that your absence leaves behind,
Shattering me in two,

192

How do you live with yourself?

Between love and fire,
This is what you wanted
Shattered pieces of you and I
You walk away and tear me down
Between goodbye and hello

Take my heart, rip it up
Kneeling at your altar,
Come to me tonight,
Our dirty secrets we will devour

Between love and fire,
This is what you wanted
Shattered pieces of you and I
You walk away and tear me down
Between goodbye and hello

Poison runs through my veins,
Leave me bleeding on the floor,
Slamming doors, haunted minds,
You walk away, but you can never leave,
Woven like fabric,
You're inside me
As I am inside you

Between love and fire,
This is what you wanted
Shattered pieces of you and I
You walk away and tear me down
Between goodbye and hello

Her eyes are glistening. The shock is evident,

and I know this song cuts her the way her words cut me that night. When I hit the last note, my voice cracks, and she turns and runs out of the arena. I drop my mic and run after her. This is not how it ends. She will not walk away from me.

"Tayla, for fuck's sake, do not fucking run away from me." This feels like déjà vu, rushing after my girl down the goddamn hallway. We come to a door, and I grasp her wrist, hauling her into the cramped storage room. I'm positive we're not meant to be in here, but I don't give a shit. She needs to hear me out.

"Callum." Her eyes latch on mine for the first time since I finished the song, and I can see the emotion etched on her exquisite face. Love. My heart thumps against my chest, and I realize this is it. I have to confess to her now.

"No. Listen. I'm tired of doing this. This back and forth has to stop. I can't do it anymore. You push, I pull. It's exhausting, and you feel it too. I want nothing more than to be yours, to have you as mine. But I can't deal with you leaving me again. Choose what you want. Because God knows—"

"I love you." Her voice is so low; I assume I imagined it. My tirade stops, and I stare at her. Mouth agape. Shocked at her admission. *She loves me? She loves me!*

"I fucking love you too." Pulling her against me, her body molds to mine. I hold onto her as if she's my salvation. My life is a joke most of the time, with the tabloids and paparazzi, but with her beside me, everything has a purpose. "Jesus, Tayla. I love you so fucking much. Last night when you walked out, you took my heart and soul with you. Ripping me in two." I cup her face in my hands and peer into her chestnut eyes. The emotion shining through is breathtaking. Obvious. Free. Beautiful. Between the love she gives me and fire she fights me with, I'm always left speechless. She's fed my innate primal hunger. Knowing I'm not alone makes me want to shout it to the world.

I lean in. My lips meet hers in a gentle, lingering kiss. It's sweet and passionate, but so damn perfect. She presses her body against mine. Her tits against my chest have me aching for her. Right here and now. "I need you." She blushes and nods. I don't need further consent. Unbuttoning my jeans, I shove them down. I watch her slip the pair of shorts she's wearing off. "Leave your panties on." Pushing my briefs to my thighs just enough to get my cock out, I rip the foil packet and sheath myself.

My hands grip her pert little ass, and I hold her against me. Her moan is linked directly to my dick because I can't think straight. I'm painfully hard.

I spin her around. With her back to me, I bend her over at the waist just as she clutches the shelving in front of her. Moving her thong to the side, I slam into her. A punishing thrust and she gasps at the invasion. She needs to be punished for leaving me. For saying goodbye. For crushing my heart.

"Callum, you're so fucking huge."

Her words add fuel to the fire, and I draw out, driving back in, hard and deep. Her whimper tells me I'm hitting that delicate edge between pain and pleasure. "Good, because you will take me. Every fucking inch of me. As you walk around during the show, you will feel me between your thighs. Do you hear me?" She nods, and I continue plunging into her. Her sweet cunt is tight and hot. My release tingles down my spine. "Baby, I need you with me. I want you to come."

I reach for her clit. My index finger circles the bud, teasing her. Her body pulses around me. Her release is close. "You will fucking scream my name."

"Yessss," she hisses, and I can hear her teeth grinding to keep from screaming until I want her to. Pulling out, I slam into her so deep. She's taking all fucking nine inches to the base, and I watch her sweet little ass slamming back onto me. My fingers strum her clit. With the thumb of my other hand, I gently circle her tight, puckered hole.

"I will take all of you. You are mine. Every fucking inch of you. This will be mine too." As the tip of my thumb slips into the back entrance of her body, she shudders and screams my name. Her molten core cinches around my shaft, sending me over the edge as I growl hers.

I am on stage. Kierra and Tayla are on the side next to the cameraman, and the crowd is wild. I mean fucking crazy. We're at the end of the set, and the whole arena is on their feet. It's incredible. I own them for the hours I'm up here. I want to finish the show with the song I wrote last night, "Between Love & Fire." The guys told me I should do it acoustically. Which I'm excited to do because it will hold everyone's attention. I planned this as her surprise, for her birthday. She needs to see I am serious about this.

As our current song ends, and I stroll over to grab my guitar. Liam and Ryan leave to hide out with the girls. The lights drop. The spotlight blinks on, and I'm lit up against the black backdrop. "How is everyone tonight?" The response is deafening. "Thank you for coming out to party with us. There's a special ending to this concert. Before I sing, I want to explain why I'm alone up here. Two months ago, I met someone. We kept it quiet, but I'm off the market now, because this girl stole my heart." There are whistles and boos, and I can't help smiling. I walk over to the microphone stand and lock it in place. I look at the front row. Eyes are locked on me, and they're hanging on my every word.

"Anyway. I fucked up a week ago. I allowed something to come between us." That's when the crowd reacts. The booing echoes throughout the arena. "Okay, okay. Listen. She didn't talk to me for a whole week. Then last night, she walked out on me. She left. Said goodbye. And she took my heart and soul with her. When the door closed, I sat, wallowed, and then wrote this. I need you to listen carefully, because let me tell you. I love her. She's beautiful, intelligent, and she is my beautifully undamaged angel. Strong, resilient, and fucking gorgeous."

The shouts that fill the arena are unbelievable. I have heard screams and squeals. But nothing prepared me for the support and love from them when I tell them the truth. "And I want to wish her a happy birthday with this song." Then I start the song that was born in pain but helped me survive and win my girl back.

TAYLA

I open my eyes to the smell of coffee. It's heaven-sent. The handsome man sitting in bed is just as ethereal. Last night was a blur. My sister arrived for the show, and we decided it would be a good idea to celebrate my birthday by getting drunk. This led us to a nightclub in Leicester Square; the name of said club eludes me in a haze of tequila. Callum had the whole crew in tow. The evening was so much fun. Emma and I chatted before the concert, which I needed after the storage room tryst with Cal.

"So, you're taking him back?" I nod. "Good. You need someone in your life, Tay. The way he looks at you is so sickeningly sweet." I chuckle at that. She's always been one for having fun, not being tied down. My sister is only turning twenty-five in two months, so she should have fun.

"I realize that, darling. I need to stop running. There is so much uncertainty. And you know I'm a jealous person." She peers at me, her eyes narrow, and I think I said something wrong when she giggles.

"Tayla Quinn, you've had it bad for Cal Hayes

since you were a teenager." My mouth falls open in shock.

"You remember that?"

"Of course! I was young, but I wasn't stupid or blind. The scrapbook you had with pics of him plastered all over it. There were other musicians, but Callum was front and center." With a wink, she chuckles at my incredulous stare.

"Does that mean you read my diary as well?" I recall hiding it with my scrapbook under my mattress, away from prying eyes. It seems I didn't do a remarkably efficient job of it.

"I know your secrets, sister." I huff at her, which earns me giggles. "Now, time for you to introduce me to that hot, sexy beast of a man who loves to bang." I look at her in shock. "The drummer!" she snickers, and I can't help joining her. God, my sister can be crude sometimes.

"Em, just be wary, Liam Hayes is not long-term boyfriend material, okay?" My warning falls on deaf ears. She's gawking at the drummer as if he's her next meal. Suddenly, I feel sorry for him rather than her.

Emma is smitten with Liam. So, I left her to it. It was adorable how she blushed every time he looked at her. She's a grown woman, and I can't treat her like a teenager anymore. There were ample times I advised her to be careful. She waved me off, convincing me she can take care of herself. Not that I thought she couldn't. I worry about her heart.

I scoot up to find Callum holding a magazine. "You into gossip now too?" I tease. When he turns the page, a sexy grin curls his lips.

"Well, when my girlfriend is in the gossip pages with my brother. Yes, I am." I snatch it from him, paging to the picture he referred to. Front and center is a half-page photograph of Liam and I hugging.

"Are you fucking serious?" I was dressed in last night's outfit — the short, black skirt and white tank top. My heels made me taller and put me at the same height as the older Hayes. He had his arm draped around my neck, and he was kissing my forehead. The caption below it read "LIAM HAYES ZEROING IN ON HIS BROTHERS GIRL." "I can't believe this," I choke incredulously. "This makes the news?" I chuck the offending book on the floor and clutch the coffee Callum left on my nightstand. Taking a leisurely sip, I savor the taste, hoping it will calm my anger at the press. I can feel him watching me silently.

"I love teasing you, Petal." Glancing at him, I find a brilliant smile.

"You were right there. I mean, you know what happened in that photo." I put my coffee cup on the nightstand and turn toward him. Lifting the sheet, I move and sit astride his lap. His hands grip my hips as I take his face in my hands. His five o'clock shadow is rough against my palms. He gives me that wicked, and my belly flip flops.

"Yes, baby. I needed to see how you handle gossip." With a soft kiss, I feel the heat between us; the taste of his lips on mine. My fingers drop to his chest, stroking the toned, smooth, warm skin. A slight shiver trembles through his body at my touch. I love knowing I have such an effect on him.

"And have I passed your test, Mr. Hayes?" He nods and scoots lower, drawing the sheet over us. I'm now lying on top of him, straddling the growing erection pressing against my core.

"Question is, can you pass the other test I have for you?" The rasp in his voice sends delicious shivers to my throbbing clit. My body pulses and my hips rock against him, eliciting a low growl. I nod and lean in, murmuring in his ear.

"Do you have so little faith in me, Hayes? I'm shocked and hurt." I kiss his neck gently, my tongue teasing the sensitive skin, moving to his chest, feathering kisses, taunting him with my mouth.

"Petal." The timbre of his tone is a sexy warning. I scoot lower until I find his beautifully chiseled V-muscles. They are prominent pointing to the thick ridge I need inside me. My eyes latch on to his; the cerulean blue now a dark, stormy sea. His hooded gaze takes in my every move. When my lips part and my tongue darts out, licking along either side of his hips, the hunger that smolders in his passionate stare turns my core to molten lava.

I tug his briefs down. His cock juts out, pointing at me. Long, beautiful, heavy, and hard.

Silky steel. Delicious. I crave to devour him. Fisting him in my palm, I stroke him in slow, measured movements. With a leisurely lick from root to tip, I flick my tongue at the crown, tasting the salty-sweet arousal as his hands fist in my hair, keeping me still. "Open, Petal. I'm going to sink into that hot, sassy mouth of yours." I see the satisfaction on his face as his hips rise and his shaft plunges into my mouth. When he hits the back of my throat, he stops. I gradually push forward, taking him past my gag reflex. "Holy fuck." His growl spurs me on, and I bob my head up and down. I repeat the move and accept him deep every time.

The salty caramel taste of him is exquisite. I crave more. I take him deep and hum my approval, sending him spiraling. His hips jerk violently, and I realize he's close. "Baby, I'm going to fill your mouth. You will swallow every fucking drop of my hot seed into that tight little throat." His crude words are hoarse, and abruptly, his shaft pulses, thickens, and the initial jet of his release shoots into my mouth. I hastily devoured all he offers, then lick him clean. His expression is filled with satisfaction.

"Did I pass the test, Mr. Hayes?" I inquire in my sweetest tone. He chuckles and sighs. Nodding, he draws me up and over him.

"Petal, you absolutely will kill me with the way you do that. My murderous, sexy minx." He moans, and I can't avoid the grin on my face. He flips us over and positions himself between my legs. The soft kisses he feathers on my neck have me quivering. He brings his mouth to my nipples, laving at the pebbled buds, teasing and tugging them between his teeth. Using his fingers on one while licking and suckling on the other. They tighten with desire, and my hips buck.

His talented mouth moves over my feverish skin until he reaches my stomach. With a soft kiss on my tattoo just below my belly button, goosebumps rise over every inch of my body. He ignores the place I need him most as he kisses my inner thighs. His beard tickles, and I'm aching for release. "Your little pussy smells incredible. Delicious, sweet nectar. All mine." Expert fingers stroke my smooth lips. "You're glistening, so beautiful." His tongue laps at the entrance to my body. When I peer down, his mouth is wet with my arousal. "So fucking amazing." He moves down again, suckling on my clit.

"Please, Callum? Fuck, please?" I beg.

Blue eyes cut a glance up, and he smirks. "What, Petal? What do you need?"

"Fuck me. Please. Goddamn it, please?" His chuckle drives me crazy. With one long lick from the bottom to the top of my pussy, he plunges two slender fingers into me. An orgasm ripples from my core, tightening deep in my belly. As he finger-fucks me, my pussy pulses around him. My body shakes violently as my release shatters through me, sending me spiraling. Stars flicker behind my eyelids as I come undone. I cry out his name. He crooks his fingers, hitting my sweet spot. My body convulses, and I clutch the sheet with a white-knuckle grip.

"That's my Petal. I need every fucking drop of your decadent nectar." He draws my release from my soul. From my core. When my belly tightens again, I think I'll pass out as I come for a second time under his wicked touch. My thighs press together, his hand trapped between them as I almost shred the sheets with my bare hands. I gradually flutter down from my orgasms, still trembling.

Suddenly, his phone buzzes. "Fuck," he cursed loudly. Ignoring it, he hovers over me, giving me a soft kiss. When it quietens, we lie in silence. "I love how you lose control with me, Petal. Every part of you is mine." His deep voice laced with lust.

"So, I passed?" My gaze is brimmed with pleasure.

"I will have to evaluate your effort, Miss Quinn, but I have to report, that was at least a B+." I reach up and bite his neck at the cocky statement, and he chuckles. "I better find out who that was." He picks up his mobile, and I see Liam's name pop up. "What the fuck does he want at this ungodly hour?"

"Emma. How are you feeling this morning?" I ask a little too loudly, and my sister winces. Cal and I walked into the restaurant and found the rest of the crew having breakfast. Kierra is on her phone. Liam and Emma are attached at the hip. Thank God they have clothes on.

"I'm okay, considering the amount of alcohol we consumed." She comes over to give me a hug and surprises me by giving Callum one too. "Nice to see you two out of bed. I hear that's where you spend most of your time." She giggles, and I can't help groaning.

"It's true." Liam's tone is gravelly from the previous night's drinking.

"Em, you should stop listening to him. He's a green-eyed monster when he doesn't get any." We sit down, and he gives me the finger.

"I got plenty last night, thank you." That earns him a group groan. The image of him and my baby sister is not what I need. Ever.

As soon as Ki ends her call, she glares at everyone, including Cal, Liam, and me. "Did I not tell you guys not to get yourselves caught on camera?"

"Ki, chill. We didn't mean to. It was an innocent kiss." We all sit quietly and wait. I think she's about to explode. Glad I'm not on the receiving end.

"Liam fucking Hayes. Can you for one moment get your fucking head out of your ass? I have to fix shit you fuck up." Her voice rises in a shrill shriek, and I stare at her in alarm. She pushes out of her chair and stalks off, leaving us all in shock.

"I'll go." Ryan jumps up and runs after her. I grab the mug of coffee the waiter places on the table and take a long sip. I'll need a gallon of caffeine to get through the day. We're headed back home tomorrow, and I'm excited to get home. That begs the question. *Was I sleeping alone? Or with Callum?*

"We need to squash this, and as soon as fucking possible. I don't want Tay in the papers." Callum's tone was sharp, and I realize why. He doesn't want my past catching up to me. At least it's only local news.

"I'm not overly worried by this. To be honest, I guess photos will appear from time to time. We have to be wary of what we're doing. I mean, it's centralized to London." I can tell from the tone of my voice I'm unsure of myself. The uncertainty that comes with our relationship is new territory. Completely. Everyone nods in agreement, and I calm.

Cal leans in and whispers in my ear, "I'm more concerned about them finding out your past. I don't want them judging you." A shiver runs down my spine. I realize it will be exposed.

"I know. We will figure it out."

"Yes." He plants a gentle kiss on my nose. "Do you want to see your parents today?"

"They're on holiday in Australia. They didn't know I would be in London, so they left before we arrived. Can we do a few touristy things?" I pout and then awarded with a sexy chuckle. Since we head back to Los Angeles tomorrow, I want to share a few of my favorite places in the city with him. Visiting in the past, I've always been with my family. Now I can share it with my boyfriend.

"Sure, Petal." Ignoring everyone, he leans in and kisses me. The groans around the table have me giggling into the kiss.

"Guys, I would like to keep my breakfast in my stomach." Liam's voice cuts through the foggy daze, and we break the kiss reluctantly.

CALLUM

Our initial stop on tour is Tower Bridge. We stand at the center overlooking the river, and I take a few hundred photos on my phone. It's windy, and her sleek, blonde hair swirls in every direction. It's good to relax; no stress from touring or the press. Her laugh is a genuine, alluring sound that trickles into my soul.

Sweet.

Melodic.

Beautiful.

Her smile is radiant, carefree, and in that moment, I know I will love her forever.

As we stroll to the Tower of London, we hold hands. Being out in public, I don't care who sees us because she's my girl. Nothing is standing in our way, and now the world knows I'm taken. I feel a weight lift from my shoulders.

I steal glances at her as we wander around, and I realize without a doubt, I want more. Since I laid eyes on her the day she spilled her coffee on me, this woman has stopped my life from spinning out of control. The echoes of her soul mingle with mine, composing a melody in my heart. Beautiful. Everlasting. Our lives are intertwined like a song, woven with lyrics, chords, and notes. I can't let her go. Not now. Not ever.

"You okay, Petal?" Chestnut pools peer at me, and a grin lights up her face.

"Yes. I guess I'm exhausted. It's been a long few weeks." I understand that. Touring isn't easy. We're headed home, and things will blow up. The media will have heard my announcement, and they'll want to meet Tayla. I hope she's ready for it.

"Let's go back to the hotel?"

"No, the Tower, then dinner." Once we reach the front of the queue, the girl behind the cash register glances up, and I see the recognition flit across her stare. *Fuck.* Pulling my hoodie up, I offer her a slight grin and pay the entrance fee. Without another word, I pull Tay along with me.

"What was that about?" She snickers, stealing glances backward at our cashier.

"She recognized me. I was making a hasty getaway." Tayla's sweet laugh resounds through the crowd, causing me to smile.

"Well, I think you're safe now. I can be your bodyguard." Another giggle escapes her beautiful plump lips. She's so perfect.

Once we board the plane, Tayla falls asleep

on my shoulder. She looks so peaceful. We're all exhausted, so I let her rest. I pull out my laptop and work on the details for the upcoming tour around the US since we have two weeks off. Then we have a few local shows. "Ki, we need to schedule a meeting with the label tomorrow. I want to finalize this album and get them off my back."

"Sure. I can call them when we land." We'll be back in LA early morning, so that will give me time to have everything finished. Once that's done, I want to plan a vacation for Tay and me. Maybe take her up to Napa for some wine tasting. A dirty weekend. My email alerts me of a new message. As soon as I open it, my body goes rigid.

I thought we heard the last from Arina. No such luck.

"I want a restraining order." I glance up at Kierra, turning my screen so she can read the message. Her face drains of color with her stare lock on mine.

"This is ridiculous." I nod in agreement. Arina is still begging me to organize a show with Gucci for her. There have been women who were selfish in using me and my fame for what they wanted. She takes the cake. I never came across someone this low. She's heard about my relationship with Tayla since I announced it to the world. "I will handle it. This little bitch is starting to seriously piss me off." Ki hates her. Even though we dated for two years, there was always an underlying tension between them. I was stupid. I know that. Leaning back, I close my eyes and try to get some sleep.

"Callum Hayes. I heard a lot about you." My eyes take in the slim woman wearing next to nothing. She's one of the models. I recognize her from the show. Liam and I spent the evening at New York Fashion week. It's frustrating needing to be seen. I was content to relax in the hotel, but my brother is happier with the five women he has hanging from his arms.

"You have?" She nods. Her manicured finger travels over my chest. It's like taking candy from a baby. No challenge. I could snap my fingers, and she will drop her panties.

"They say you have a beautiful . . . voice?" Her other hand falls to my crotch. My dick thickens at her touch. With a gulp, I down my drink and grasp her wrist and haul her backstage.

"You want my cock?" My rough growl in her ear has her body trembling.

"I do." I lift the hem of her dress, tugging it up, finding her naked beneath. A slow stroke of her slick, bare cunt has my shaft throbbing.

"You're already dripping for me?" My index finger slides into her with ease. She's tight. Hot. Wet. Just how I like them. The buzz of the champagne, wine, and beer has me aching to drive into her.

"Fuck me. Any way you choose." Her words are fuel to my raging hard-on. I pull my finger from her and drop my zipper. With the foil wrapper on the floor, I sheath myself and slam into this little slut. Fuck. Her body cinches my thick erection. I draw out slowly and plunge in deeper, leaving her breathless.

"That's it; take my fucking dick. You wanted a rock star to fuck you."

"Yes, fuck me!" Her cries are loud. Bringing my hand up, I cover her mouth as I ram into her. Her whimpers are muffled. Her legs tighten around my waist, pulling me in. My release is close, and when her eyes roll back, and her cunt squeezes me, my body goes rigid, and I fill the rubber.

As soon as I slip out of her, I discard the condom in the trash. Her green eyes glisten up at me. I recognize the emotions that are always there. Desire. Lust. Need. Once her dress is smooth, and I am tucked in my pants, we make our way out to the party. My brother's stare settles on me — his eyebrow quirks in question. I don't acknowledge him. Strolling to the bar, I order a drink. Once I have another beer, I down it in one deep swallow. "Here's my number, rock star. Call me if you want a repeat performance."

With a wink, she leaves a napkin with her number written in bright red lipstick. Against my better judgment, I push it in my pocket.

My eyes crack open as soon as the plane is coming into land. My mind is reeling from the dream. It was too real. My past wasn't the brightest, and the things Arina and I did were constantly on the subtle line between right and wrong. I never did drugs, though. My brother, on the other hand, did. Kierra's stare is burning a hole into me. When I meet her gaze, I realize she's worried about Arina.

"I emailed our PR. They'll issue a statement about you and Tayla. Then we can have the restraining order delivered. You know there will be retaliation?" I nod. I need that woman out of my life, and this shit has to stop. My life is finally where I want it to be. With a delicate caress on my woman's cheek, her eyelashes flutter, and I'm met with deep chestnut.

"We've landed." She grins, and my heart soars. Nothing can prepare you for the moment love strikes. She has captured my splintered soul and filled the cracks with her love. My sweet, damaged angel.

"Hey." Her voice is heavy with sleep. When she straightens, I miss her body against mine.

"Hey, gorgeous." Planting a soft, chaste peck on her lips, I rise, clutching our bags. Lacing my fingers with hers, we disembark. I leave the crew to pack the trunk. Liam, Kierra, Ryan, Tayla, and I step into the arrivals section of the airport, and we are hounded by the press. A few hundred people are yelling and hollering. The flashes are blinding, and I immediately pull my hoodie up. Tay follows suit, and we are led by security through to our waiting car.

"That was unbelievable."

"It was. Guess they've learned about my current relationship status." With a roll of her eyes, she peers at me. Pulling her against me, I wrap my arms around her. The desire to touch her is a persistent ache.

"Bro, you've upset a few million women. It's okay. I'm ready to help them overcome the disappointment." Liam's chuckle earns him a scowl from both girls. "What? I'm joking."

"You better be kidding, Hayes. Or you can deal with my sister." My brother and Emma hit it off in London, and when she arrives back here in a month, I expect his hands will be full trying to deal with her. Both Quinn sisters are little sticks of dynamite.

"Tayla, understand this. There are things I will do to her. Things to make her forget she was angry with me." The smirk on his face is evidence whatever is running through his mind is filthy. It's something I don't need to know. Or be privy to imagining.

"Bro, seriously. We do not need visuals." Laughter echoes throughout the car. We're pulling up to the house moments later. There's something I have to ask my girl, and I hope she will not deny me. My phone rings as we step into the living room. A quick glance at the screen tells me this isn't good. I don't want to take the call, but ignoring her will only anger her. "Hayes." With a smile, I leave Tayla and stroll outside. "What?"

"Do not take my threat lightly, Callum. Your help in landing the Gucci show is vital for me. I have to walk for them. Make it happen." Arina's voice grates my nerves, but there's nothing I can do until the press release is ready. Stalling her is my only option. This is ridiculous.

"You know I can't do this anymore. It's done. Over. Do you not understand? I'm in a relationship."

"Twenty-four hours." Her words are venomous, and the poison runs through my veins. There will be consequences if I don't follow through. Knowing the woman on the other end is a snake, I shudder to think what she has up her sleeve. The restraining order is imperative; then she can disappear.

"Fuck you." The line goes dead. I feel eyes on me, and when I turn, I come face to face with Tay. Her gaze holds questions. *Do I tell her?* A decision needs to be made quickly because this is it. She will not let it go. I can see it in her eyes. The last time I kept a secret from her, she left me. Now, I choose to do it right. Honesty is the best policy. *Right?*

TAYLA

I stand there, staring at him. Waiting. The indecision in his eyes makes me realize something is wrong. Terribly wrong. The question is, will he trust me enough to tell me? "Cal?"

"Darling, let's sit. I need to talk to you." Those words tug at my heart more than I want them to. There's an ache deep inside my chest I never want to feel. *Was he breaking up with me?* This must be about his ex. *Shit. Shit. Shit.*

"Arina is demanding I help her get into a show. I had done it before when I was seeing her. She's capable of fucking with my life if I don't do it. Nothing exists between her and me. I told her to fuck off. My concern is that she may force my hand." The fear seeps into my veins. The icy shiver that runs through my body is too much to handle. I rise abruptly and turn away from him. She could dig into my past and find what I did. She could easily break us up and have Callum back in her life. If I leave, then maybe she won't have anything to hold over him.

"I should go. It's easier if I'm gone. Just give

her what she wants for now. Once I'm away from here, from you, then you won't have to worry about her finding out about my job at the club. What if she finds out about him? He could ruin your life."

"The fuck you are. There's no way in hell I'm letting you walk out that door. Do you hear me? And that fucking dick who hurt you, he should try and come after me. He will be fucking sorry he was ever born." He's behind me in an instant. With his arms circling me, the tears flow. As soon as I blink, they fall, my cheeks wet with the ache of putting him through this.

"Callum. She's forcing you to do this because of me." His hold tightens around me. Protecting me in ways he doesn't even know. "She knows we're together."

"That's why we will fix it."

"I can't ask you to."

"You're not asking. I'm telling you." I love him with all I am. *Is there a way we can make it through this?* He grips my shoulders and turns me to face him. Our eyes latch on each other. The emotion is unmistakable. Screaming at me. Love. Nothing else. There's no doubt in his gaze. My heart stutters for a second. This is real. I have no choice. Leaving is pointless. I'll never survive without him. "Baby, you listening?"

"What?" Had he been talking?

"I said we need to talk to Ki and the guys. You're not leaving. That's for damn sure." I smile. Nodding, I lean up on my tiptoes and kiss him on his cheek. His day-old stubble tickles my lips.

"Okay." With an arm circling my waist, he tugs me into the house with him. "Everyone, there's something you should know." Ryan and Liam turn toward us, and Kierra gives me a slight smile of encouragement. My racing heart calms considerably; Her expression shows all I needed. I'm part of their family. The story about what happened with him affects me every day. But I have Callum.

"What's up, bro?"

"Arina wants me to get her into the Gucci show. Since she's history, I told her to fuck off. You know what she's like."

"Yeah, a fucking roach." Liam's dislike for this girl runs deep.

"Cal, I recall you've had shit with her for a while. What can we do?" Ryan flops onto the sofa. With a grin, his eyes dart between the two of us. "Do you need me to drop kick her?" It's true. He's an enormous guy. Standing six feet tall, he's taller than Callum. His broad shoulders make him scarier. The only thing that makes him approachable is his smile. It's especially charming. His personality matches. The all-round nice guy. He's the joker of the group. He and Liam love pranking the crew, which is amusing.

"So, let's fucking dump her in a hole someplace." Liam's chuckle masks it, but I expect he's serious. At the start of my relationship with

Cal, he didn't trust me, but when his gaze lands on me now, the smile he gives is sincere. "Don't worry, darling, that little fame whore will be history soon."

"Thank you. There is something I have to confess. About me. Callum knows, and it's taken me a while to pluck up the courage to talk about it. Since I'm not allowed to leave." I peer at my boyfriend, who grins in response. "I should be honest. When I was studying, my parents had just left to go to the UK. My dad had lost his fortune to his business associate. When the offer arrived from the insurance company for him to have a permanent job, he accepted. We were bankrupt. I was sleeping on my classmate's sofa. She was the one who got me a position at the place she worked — a part-time gig. I needed money. For my apartment. For school. My father luckily paid most of my schooling before he lost everything. I lacked the basics. Books, food, you get the idea." My glance settles on each person in the room. Callum's grip on me tightens. It's comforting. He supports me. "I ended up dancing. It was an upmarket club. I did aerial yoga, and the owner thought it would be a distinct performance to bring in the crowd."

I take a sharp breath. "Anyway. I didn't strip. Or fuck anyone." I cringe at my words. Everyone is silent. "So, I danced and paid for my apartment. I studied. There was a guy, a patron. He got . . . Attached. I . . . There wasn't anything I could do. He . . . I . . ." The story tumbles from my mouth. Nobody moves, and tears streak my face. Suddenly, Liam bolts to his feet, capturing me in a bear hug. We stand silently. My body relaxes in his arms. My tears stain his T-shirt. Everything seems too much.

He leans in and mumbles, "So, do we get a private show?"

"Fuck off, Liam," Callum groans. I peer at my boyfriend, his eyes shining with annoyance.

Ignoring his brother, Liam carries on. "Look, Tayla, darling. This is not as bad as you think. You shouldn't be ashamed of what you've done. We make mistakes, and we do things we aren't proud of, but my brother loves you. So do we." For the first time since I met Liam Hayes, he stares at me with heartfelt affection. There's something so surreal having one of the world's hottest men convincing you that you are a part of his family.

We're on our way to Salt Lake City. We've been driving for five hours, another four to go, maybe five. The bus is spacious, but not enough. I'm tired, grumpy, and in need of a hot shower. This is the first local show Hunter's is playing, and I'm intrigued to see how the crowd handles them. Or vice versa. My body hurts. I roll over in the small bunk bed and peer over at Callum. He's been asleep for the last hour, and I'm tempted to wake him for a cuddle.

"I can see you." His raspy voice sends a tingle down my spine.

"How can you see me?" I lean up and whisper in his ear.

"Because your eyes are burning a hole into me. You realize it's creepy watching me while I sleep?" he murmurs. Our hushed whispers are low in the silence of the bus. The rest of the band are only a few feet away.

"It's not creepy when you aren't sleeping, is it?" When his normally sky-blue gaze locks on me and turns a stormy grey, my belly somersaults. I reach down and find him rock hard in his sweats. With a squeeze, he pulses in my grip. A crooked grin curls his perfect lips.

"You are a very naughty girl, Tayla." Desire is thick in his growl as he pulls me on top of him. Our bodies align perfectly. I can't sit up since the beds allow little room, but I straddle him. His soft, smooth hands run up my back, moving over to my chest. When his thumbs tease my nipples, an electric current shoots straight to my clit. The rough pads flick over my pebbled buds, sending shock waves of pleasure through me. "Mmmm, my baby is turned on for me."

"Always, Cal, you know that." I lean in, and our lips mold together. A fusion of yearning. I suck his bottom lip into my mouth. The sweet flavor of the orange juice he had only hours before mixed with the flavor of him is intoxicating. My teeth graze his full lips, and a groan rumbles in his throat. The vibration is trembling through me.

"Can you be quiet?" he questions hoarsely. I nod quickly. He's about to fuck me. Hard. Fast. And there's nothing I want more than him inside me. His eyes fall to my lips, bruised from the rough kiss. We fumble with condom wrappers and clothes until he is sliding into me. The thick, solid shaft filling me like no other man ever will has me whimpering. Somehow, Callum flips me over and is now hovering over me. His slow, deep thrusts have me chewing my lower lip to keep from moaning out loud. My legs are wrapped around him, and my head drops onto the pillow as he slams into me, hitting that spot that has my toes curling.

My nails dig into his back. Our mouths collide in hungry kisses. His tongue licks into me. Devouring. Tasting. Consuming. A frenzy of pleasure and desire burn through my veins, tightening my core. My orgasm coils within me as my pussy clenches, milking his release, my mouth comes down on his shoulder. My teeth sink in until I taste blood. Callum's feral growl is a primal, base sound. Animalistic in every sense. I feel a sharp sting as he bites into the sensitive skin of my neck, sucking hard, marking me. I know there'll be a bruise later.

There are moments in your life; you wonder why something happens. This was one of those occasions. The events of tonight will forever be a mystery. *Why? How?* I'm standing in the VIP section of the Meet & Greet with Ki. The boys are signing autographs and taking photos with VIP ticket holders. Watching them interact with the fans is the same as seeing them with friends. They regard each person with the utmost respect. Since the European tour, I've become used to Callum with the female fans.

It's only until I recognize Arina walking up does my world swirl, and bile rises in my throat. "What the fuck is she doing here?" The venom in my voice surprises me.

"Fuck." Kierra's response gives me the indication she didn't know about the impromptu visit either. She walks up to the band, and Callum's face falls into a sneer. He leans in and whispers in her ear. It can't be good, because her expression contorts into an unpleasant grimace. It's as if I'm having an out-of-body experience. There's nothing I can do to stop the next few minutes from playing out.

In slow motion, she turns toward him. Her arm reaches up to his chest, and a metallic glint shines in the dim light. Two bodyguards grab at her, but her hand makes contact. Callum crumples, and that's when I see blood. The icy chill that flows through my veins burns, and my heartbeat deafens me as it pounds in my ears. No amount of self-control can stop you from wanting to crawl to that person and burrow yourself inside of them. Into their very soul.

Kierra's scream rips me from the horrific scene in front of me. Willing my legs to move, I bolt to the man I love. He's on the floor, gripping his ribs. When I hear the anguished cries, I wonder who it is. Only when strong arms surround me, do I realize it's coming from me. Liam's got a hold on me while the medics rush to treat his brother. He's pulling me away. I try to fight, but I can't. I need to be there. I have to see him. Touch him. *Why is Liam pulling me away?*

"Doll face, calm down." Liam's body is shaking with anger. It vibrates off him in waves. "That little whore is gone. I would love to rip her apart, but you need to calm down." His words sink in slowly. My throat is ragged. "Tay, you need to stop screaming." Glaring up into hazel eyes, I realize in my shocked state that my throat is raw. Someone hands me a bottle of water, and Liam pulls me back to the seats and sets me down. I can't watch them work on Callum's bleeding body. Averting my gaze, I stare absentmindedly at the carpet.

"Liam . . ." My voice is soft, raspy. His caramel eyes drop to mine. "Is he . . .?"

"He will be okay. I promise. That bitch, however, will not be fine. That I swear to you."

It's a dizzying pain. I am sitting in the back of an ambulance. The lights, noise, and the words I don't understand. Why are they saying critical? What do they mean? My body is rocking back and forth. Liam and Kierra are in the car behind us. Everything is a blur. Blood, lots of blood; it's all I see. Red. Pain. Searing pain. They mention poison. Why? What's going on? "Ma'am?" I glance up. The medic is staring at me. "Drink this." He hands me a glass. The water inside is murky. Cloudy. "It will help."

Nodding, I gulp the bitter-tasting liquid. Medication. I don't want to sleep. Why are they making me sleep? "What is this?"

"It's for shock. You've been through a lot." I don't answer him. I can't. He doesn't know. How can he? Maybe he does. My head is spinning, and I feel sleepy. Hands guide me down. "Sleep. We'll get you both to the hospital soon."

My snap eyes open. I glare up at a white ceiling. My body is rigid, and my head feels heavy. *Shit! Callum!* Jumping up, I glance around. My eyes fall on the hospital bed, where the man I love is lying. He's connected to tubes. There's a heart rate monitor beeping. *Thank god it's beeping.* "Tay." I turn my stare toward the voice I know. Liam.

"Is he . . .? What's happening?" I stand and walk over to the bed. Reaching out, I tentatively touch his hand. There are so many tubes. Tears prick my eyes, but I blink them away.

"He's going to be okay. They said he had toxins in his system; they had to flush it out."

"Why didn't you wake me?" My glare lands on caramel eyes.

"You needed rest." Just then, the door opens, and I come face to face with Mrs. Hayes. "Mother, this is Tayla. She's the new sound engineer." He doesn't introduce me as Callum's girlfriend. Maybe he wants Cal to do it.

"It's nice to meet you, darling." Her smile is affectionate and warm.

"And you too."

"Tay, let's get coffee." I reluctantly follow Liam out to the hallway. "I didn't say anything to her. I wasn't sure what you or Cal would want to tell her." Nodding, I offer a small smile.

"It's okay. I don't think this is the right time anyway." My body is shaking. I don't realize it until Liam places a hand on my shoulder.

"You're tired. You need to rest some more."

"I can't, Liam. He's in there, hurt. It's my fault."

"How do you figure it's your fault? It's that crazy bitch's fault. Tayla, my brother loves you. I haven't ever seen him care for another woman like he does for you."

"You're not the asshole I thought you were." My eyes meet his, but there is a wickedness that burns inside those caramel orbs.

"Oh, darling, I am an asshole. Trust me. If he weren't so in love with you, I would have fucked you already."

"God, you can be such a dickhead, Liam Hayes." As I reach up to slap him, he grabs my wrist.

"Go get yourself a coffee. I'm going to take my mother to her store now so she can check on the staff. You can have time alone with my brother." He turns and walks away. I spin on my heel and make my way to the coffee machine. My body is shaking — with pain, anger, and frustration. Liam Hayes is an asshole. His brother, on the other hand, is the love of my life.

Once I have a coffee in hand, I make my way to Cal's room. Nothing's changed. He's just lying there, not moving. "Cal, handsome. I need you. You have to wake up. Please?" The tears I've been holding onto spill over and run down my face. The ache in my heart knocks me breathless. I need him. I can't lose him.

He pushed his way into my life. He reached inside me, grabbed my heart, and filled it with love. Freeing me of the pain and anguish I was holding onto. He helped me release those feelings and find love. There's no way I can lose that. My tears don't run dry. I realize they'll only stop when he opens his eyes, and I can once again stare into their depths and feel safe.

"Callum. I love you. More than life. More than my next breath. You're my rock star and my bad boy. I can't lose you. Your voice lulls my pain and tears, and your hands caress and care. Your body takes me higher than I ever thought I could go. But most importantly, your heart has intertwined with mine. We're one person, handsome. And if anything happens to you, it happens to me too." Leaning forward, I place my head beside his hip, holding onto his soft, smooth hand, and my eyes drift closed.

CALLUM

The last thing I remember is excruciating pain. There was only one sound that pierced through the cacophony of voices and noise, and that was Tayla screaming, crying, but I couldn't get to her. When I move, hands press me down — holding me in place. My breathing is heavy. My eyes feel as if they're glued shut. Heat sears in my chest, making it difficult to think straight.

"Callum . . . Can you hear me?" *Petal? Baby? Fuck. Why can't I open my mouth?*

"He's alert. We need to wait it out. There was a poisonous substance on the blade he was stabbed with, so he will be disorientated. The blade missed all major arteries, and we managed to rid his body of toxins. He's lucky. He may be in and out for a day or so, but he will wake up."

"Okay, I'll stay." The room falls silent. *Where is she? Tay?* This is ridiculous. The pain pulses in my ribs and arm burning through my body. In my veins.

"Cal, I'm here. The doctor said I should talk to you. So, well, you scared me shitless. You realize you can't leave me. My heart won't take that. You have to wake up, okay? Do you hear me, Hayes?" Her fingers lightly caress my hand. It soothes the burn. It's soft and smooth. "Your mother is here. She's gone to grab a coffee. Liam and Ryan too. Ki is trying to sort out the press release to cancel the rest of the shows. Your mom is nice, but I didn't tell her about us yet. I mean. I wasn't sure. You know . . ." Her voice cracks. She's crying. Fuck, I want to hold her. Her hand trembles over mine and the emotion in a simple touch is extraordinary. It takes every ounce of my concentration to will my eyes to open. I need to see her. *Fucking torture. My Petal.*

"You will never leave me. Do you hear me?"
"What are you doing here, Arina?" Her eyes are dark, glossy. She's drunk. Or something. Walking over to the window, I take in the view. We're not in LA. That much is obvious. I don't remember how I got here.
"We are meant to be together, Cal. You know how perfect we are. I am yours. Forever. You promised." Spinning around, I glare at the woman I once thought I loved. That was unfortunately, not love. I know, because I love someone now. And she's not standing in front of me.
"There isn't an us. I do not want you. I will never be yours. No way in hell. Do you understand me? You are a fucking fame whore. You've used me for the last time," I spit at her. The wince in her expression is evident. It doesn't faze me she's hurt by my words. She has taken from me. Never again. I am

not a charity. My heart is thudding against my chest.

Her face contorts in pain — pure, agonizing torture. I stare into cold, calculating eyes. Realizing nothing will make me want her. Or the life we had. "Leave. Now."

Loud beeps pull me from my fuzzy mind. When my eyes snap open, everything is distorted. Blinking hurts. *What the fuck?* "Petal." The word is ragged. My throat is parched and scratchy.

"Cal?" Turning my head, I'm greeted with glossy, chestnut pools filled with love. My vision dims. "Callum. Look at me?" Her hands on my face are tender and compassionate. Soft. Loving. Calming. Our eyes meet. I blink rapidly. She's here. My beautiful angel. My vision is still blurred, and it's as if I'm floating, but she grounds me.

"Baby, what happened?" The tubes in my arms hold me in place as my gaze rakes over the room. It's empty except for Tayla, me, and the bed I'm in.

"You're in the hospital. You have been for three days. Arina stabbed you. Before the concert. She hurt you. Security caught and arrested her. I think they said she would be admitted into a psychiatric hospital. I couldn't focus on the rest." My body aches, but the searing pain has passed. "Lie back, handsome." Her voice is a salve to my heart and soul.

"Are you okay?"

"You're in the hospital, and you ask me if I'm okay?" Her giggle is music to my ears. Better than any song I've ever written.

"I worry about you. Even in my delirious, drugged-up state, you're inside me." It was true; she's woven deep in the intricate fabric of my being. Seeping into the tiny fractures and filling them with joy.

"I'm fine. Seeing you like that. Just . . . lying there, not moving. I didn't know what to do. If it wasn't for Liam . . . There was a moment I thought I lost you. It was scary. What would I have done?"

"I'm here, baby. Don't be scared. I won't leave you. You're stuck with my sorry ass."

"You mean sexy ass?" She giggles, and I can't help grinning. The perfection of my girl is breathtaking.

"Yes, yours is pretty sexy." Her cheeks pinken, and I crave to make her blush forever. The sight makes my heart fill with emotion. I wish I knew how to ask her. It needs to be perfect. The pressure I used to have with other girls is absent when I'm with Tayla. She's exquisite in a natural way. There's nothing fake about her, and sometimes I feel as if my world is the fictitious part of us.

"Cal?" Her anxious gaze darts to my face and the machines, and I realize my heart rate has spiked.

"I'm okay. Baby, I want to introduce you to my mother. As my girlfriend. When I get out of here." Her eyes are wide showing she's nervous. It's written all over her face. "She needs to meet the woman I love." Her face brightens in a smile.

"Okay. We can do that. Do you want some water?" I nod and watch her grab the glass. Pushing the straw towards my mouth, she helps me take a few cooling sips. I can't wait to have her meet my mother.

We're walking toward the door of my childhood home as nerves get the better of me. I haven't in my thirty-five years done this with a girl. The uncertainty has me on edge. If I had the foresight to know what will happen once we step inside, I'd be able to calm down. Nothing has prepared me for this. Not standing in front of a few hundred thousand people. Not world fame.

Our hands are linked. I can sense her gaze on me. "Are you okay, Cal?" I nod, the tension has to be radiating from me. I realize she must sense it. We have such an innate connection. Her emotions are distinct; I feel them when she does.

"I will be."

"Is she going to hate me? I mean, I didn't tell her at the hospital. Should I have? I didn't think it was appropriate." I plant a quick kiss on her lips to quiet her. Turning, I grasp the large antique knocker. It booms on the large wooden door. As it slides open, we are greeted with one of the most exquisite women in my life.

"My rock star." Her voice is calm, but the emotion is thick and washes over me. The wince on my face when she pulls me in for a hug doesn't go unnoticed, and her face falls. "You still in pain, darling?"

"A little. It will be okay. There's someone I need you to meet. Officially." Her gaze falls behind me to the blonde beauty standing patiently in my shadow. A place I never want Tayla; she belongs beside me.

"Hello."

"Tayla, my mom." My girl steps forward, and my mother embraces her in an affectionate hug. The most remarkable women in my world are in one place. My heart is overflowing with love, and I can't find words to add more to the introduction.

"It's lovely to meet you, Mrs. Hayes." A soft blush pinkens Tayla's cheeks. Her nervous demeanor will soon diminish. The concept of me having a girlfriend is so very new to my mother that when her grey eyes settle on mine, the surprise is apparent.

"Please, call me Abigail. You make me sound older than I am. It's so nice to finally meet the girl who has stolen my baby's heart." I groan at the term baby. She loves embarrassing me, and I realize this is the day she's been waiting for my whole life.

"A pleasure Abigail."

"And you, darling. I can understand why

my Cal is so smitten by you. It's about time he brought a girl home." Rolling my eyes, I huff and glare at her. They giggle as if they now share a secret joke.

"Are you two about done? Mother, I didn't bring her here for you to gang up on me," I grumble behind them.

"Oh, I realize that Callum. I love making you squirm." She smiles, hooking her arm through Tay's, and they head off toward the kitchen with me trailing behind. I knew she would love Tayla as much as I do. "Tay, tell me how my son roped you into dating him? Because he's a hard nut to crack." Another groan rumbles through my chest. This will be a long day.

We're sitting at the long patio table enjoying a glass of wine and lunch. My mother and Tayla hit it off instantly as they've been talking for hours. I'm not exaggerating. I'm happy to see the two women in my life smile, laugh, and gossip about me. And no, they're not bothered that I'm seated a few feet away. I haven't loved another woman before, other than my mom. To feel the love I do for Tay is overwhelming. There was always an essential part of me missing, and my heart was incomplete. Fissures that seemed barren. The loneliness caught me at the most inopportune times.

Sitting in my car, on the sofa watching

television, even just sleeping, was difficult. Not having someone there when you wake up. Or when you fall asleep. It's a slow poison that oozes into your veins and grabs hold of you. Since I found Tay, I'm complete. I realize I don't have to be alone. Now all I desire is to make her mine forever. When she heads to the restroom, I glance at my mother. "I'm going to ask her next week."

"I'm happy for you, darling. You have no idea how thrilled I am you've found love. Be good to each other. I know you will, but always be wary of each other's feelings. Don't hurt each other and make her smile every day."

"I plan to. Her smile is the only thing that gets me through my darkness, Mom." The smile on her face is one of pride. To see her proud of me never fails to make me happy. Both Liam and I aren't, or haven't been perfect sons, but we're trying.

"Good. Now I hope I will be getting some grandbabies real soon."

"Mother, please. Let's just take it one day at a time." She offers me a conspiratorial smile and sips her wine innocently. The idea of Tayla carrying my child has my cock pulsing behind my zipper. She would look incredible. Her beautiful face glowing. Jesus, I need to calm down. Or I will be sitting here with a fucking hard-on.

TAYLA

"Callum, this is absurd. You need to tell me where we're going. You've been acting strange since the shows have been cancelled. I don't even know what to pack."

Glancing over at my insanely annoying and sexy rock star, I find his cerulean eyes are glistening with mischief. After the lunch with Abigail, he's been up to something. That was such a perfect day. Getting to meet the woman who raised the man who now holds my heart.

"Petal, I told you. We are heading to a special place, and if you ask me again, I will blindfold you, throw you over my shoulder, spank your sexy little ass, and chuck you in my trunk. That way, you won't be able to see where we are headed."

"Callum Hayes! And you kiss your mother with that mouth?"

"You know it, baby." With a mischievous wink, he leaves me in the bedroom with empty suitcases. It's only been a week since I met his mom, but she's called me a few times. I want

Callum to meet my parents. They'll love him; however, my dad might give him grief. *But isn't that what dads do?*

I spend the next fifteen minutes throwing almost everything I own into the suitcases on the bed. When my luggage is brimming with clothes, I zip it up. "Are you ready, Petal?" Callum is standing at the door, staring at me with an amused expression.

"I guess so. I didn't have a clue what to pack, so I pretty much included my whole closet." He's so good at surprising me. I haven't one inkling on where we're heading. He can be so fucking frustrating. I guess that's why I love him. He's constantly keeping me on my toes, but I give as good as I get.

"That's fine. If there's something you forgot, which I am sure there won't be, we can buy it. Come on." With a tug, he pulls my suitcase along behind him as we make our way to the living room. Ki and Liam are working on their laptops when we walk in.

"Are you all set, doll?" She grins.

"I guess so. Not sure where I'm ready to go to though." My dig at Callum goes unnoticed.

"You'll love it. I promise." The secret is making me crazy. My eye roll catches his attention. He leans in, his hot breath on my neck.

"Do that again, and you will be squealing when I get you alone." His words are a low hiss that send heat straight between my legs. Straightening, he turns to his brother and Kierra.

"We'll be back in a week. If you need anything, just call."

We say our goodbyes and head to the garage. The SUV is filled with luggage, and soon, we're heading down the highway. As we pass the familiar sights, I realize he's driving to the airport. A brief peek at Cal makes me smile. His profile is rugged, sexy, and the stubble that hints on his jaw has me squirming. His expression is serious as he concentrates on the road. I want to ask, but he won't tell me. At least I know our destination is the airport.

"We're flying? I don't have my passport."

"Petal, do you think I would not have everything planned? I packed it. When you were in the shower." In a smooth, swift move, he lifts my hand and places a soft kiss on my knuckles. This man truly is incredible in every way.

"You do realize this is kidnapping." His laughter fills the car, and the sparkle in those sky-blue eyes is obvious with amusement.

"It's only kidnapping if I blindfold you and tie you up. Now that right there sounds like a brilliant idea. We could have some fun with that." I gape at him incredulously.

We pull up to the departures long-term parking area, and Cal parks in the assigned spot. We're met by a few security to assist with our luggage and escort us to the gate. We board the plane moments later. I settle into my window seat, which he always offers me. I love watching the clouds go by. "This will be a long flight,

Petal."

We're in business class, but I haven't heard where we're headed since Callum forced my earbuds in and proceeded to block out any announcements the pilot made. I shift to face him. My stomach whirls as the pilot takes us down the runway, and quickly we're in the air. "Callum, where are we flying to?"

"I assure you; you will love it. Just sit back. Enjoy it. Or would you like me to help you relax?" His sky-blue gaze darkens with the hidden promise in his words. Squirming in the seat, I smirk at him. The hooded stare that's burning a hole into me sends heat to my pussy.

"Now that sounds like an illicit question, Hayes."

"Trust me, baby, it's a dirty promise." Desire tightens the knot in my core. My panties have disintegrated. The smirk that tugs on the side of his mouth is wicked, and I crave those lips on every inch of my body.

"Then you better keep your word." Lust is heavy in my tone. He reaches up, trailing the line of my jaw, leaving goosebumps in their wake. With his index finger sliding between the swell of my breasts, he teases the soft skin, earning him a slight whimper.

"I intend to keep that vow and many more." With a slow, torturous movement, he drops a hand into the waistband of my shorts and finds my soaked underwear. A deep, sexy growl reverberates through his chest. "Fuck." The phrase is so dark and delicious falling from his mouth. It's decadent and washes over me like hot wax drizzled on taut skin.

He caresses me through the flimsy fabric covering my bare pussy. The expert touch is sending me reeling. My head drops backward, and my eyes flutter closed. "Look at me, Petal. I need you to see what your whimpering does to me." My eyes snap open, locking on his. Slender fingers nudge the material aside, finding my slick, heated core. Circling my clit, in slow firm movements, he watches me. The reaction on my face spurring him on. The throb is unbearable. My hand involuntarily grips his bicep, digging my nails in as I near the edge.

"Not yet." He stops teasing my hardened bundle of nerves and drives two fingers into me. The action is slow, taunting me, keeping me dangling on edge. Just the way he prefers it. He wants me to be a whimpering mess, and then he sends me spiraling. The pleading must be apparent in my eyes because he offers me a devilish smile, which coils desire deep in my stomach. He eases out of me. "Now, if you stop pouting about where we're going, I will think about allowing you an orgasm."

My mouth drops open, and I stare at him incredulously. That's unbelievable. "Callum, please? You can't leave me like this." A wicked glint flashes over his face. The flight attendant comes to ask if we would like anything. *Yes, I need a fucking orgasm.* I want to scream. My body

241

is tingling. My pussy is drenched, and he sits there as if nothing is troubling him.

I don't hear him ordering the drinks with my mind clouded with lust. I notice we're alone again. Blue eyes flicker over me. The heat in his gaze sears me. My skin prickles and the ache between my legs is becoming unbearable. "Cal," I hiss. "You're being ridiculous."

"Don't worry, Petal. You'll get what you crave soon enough." The hostess returns with our ordered drinks. He hands me mine, and he draws a long sip of his beer. His one hand falls to my thigh, causing me to jump. He brings it up toward my core, stopping short of the place I want it. "Will you be quiet?" My gaze darts around anxiously, and even though we're in business class and it's not as busy, there are other passengers on board. My desire for release is overwhelming, and I nod. "Good girl."

His fingers trail over my material-clad pussy. A soft whimper escapes my lips. "If you can't be silent, you have to sit in agony the whole flight." Sucking my bottom lip between my teeth, I peer at him.

Those smooth fingers slide into the leg of my shorts and nudge my panties to the side. He rubs my now tortured bundle of nerves, and my nails dig into the seat. My head falls back, and my eyes flutter closed. "Petal, what did I tell you about looking at me?"

Snapping my eyes toward him, I lock my gaze with his. He continues to finger-fuck my pussy slowly. He leans toward me. His lips on my ear, hot breath on my neck. "I love feeling your tight little cunt around my fingers, my tongue, and especially my cock." His crude words mixed with the way he crooks both digits against my sweet spot send me spiraling. An orgasm rips into me, and I bite my lower lip until the metallic taste of blood floods my mouth.

My body trembles in the wake of my release. As I descend from my blissful high, Callum pulls his fingers from my core. I watch him bring them to his mouth, licking each one. His eyes close as he savors the taste. "Fuck, I love your nectar. It's heaven, my angel. You taste like honey." The erotic gesture has me clamping my thighs. The insatiable ache he has brought to my body is never-ending.

"So do you, handsome. Remember, there's a time and place for everything, and payback is sweet. And when I do, you'll definitely be speechless." His stormy gaze meets mine. I lean forward, my lips whispering in his ear, "I want to take your big, hard cock deep into my throat. Sucking you into my hot mouth, flicking and teasing you with my tongue. Then make you feed me every drop of your hot seed. Then lick your beautiful cock clean." My dirty words have the effect I was hoping for. The groan that rumbles in his chest is low and sexy. A growl. It's animalistic. My hand trails up his thigh. Reaching his crotch, I feel the thick, hard ridge behind his zipper.

"Petal, you better behave, or you'll get fucked right here with everyone watching." Without another word, I stand, scoot past him, and walk toward the restrooms. With a quick glance at him, I blow a kiss to his astonished expression. Before I can lock the door, it's pushed open, and Callum walks in, hovering over me. The only sound is a small click.

No words are spoken, and we're tearing at each other's clothes. He pulls off my shorts and panties in one swift move. My fingers are undoing the button on his jeans, and I tug at the zipper. "Callum . . ." His name on my lips stops him dead. "I want you . . ." My words trail off, and I don't know how to say it.

"That is the plan here, baby."

"No, I mean. I . . . Um . . ."

"Tay, what? Tell me?"

"I need to feel you without a condom." My eyes dart up at him and find his hooded stare, hungry, and feral. "I'm on the pill." That's the only permission he needs. With a tight grip on my ass, he lifts me against him. This has me wrapping my legs around his waist.

"I have no idea how long I can last feeling you bare on my shaft, baby. But I will make it up to you." The emotion in his gaze holds me hostage, and I can't break free. I don't want to. Ever. A small nod and he's sliding into me.

It's slow, and the pleasure that shoots through my body scorches my skin. The silky steel of his erection is exquisite against my heated walls. I'm slick with arousal, and he slips in effortlessly, stretching me wide. "Jesus, Petal, I can't go slower. This will be one fast and hard fuck." My hands twine behind his neck as his hips slam against me.

Our mouths fuse in a searing kiss. His tongue fucks my mouth as his cock fucks my pussy. My belly tightens; my release is close. Coiling, twisting, curling my toes, shattering my senses.

Even though we're in a cramped restroom, the emotion in the air is erotic, romantic, and filled with passion. My heart soars with his. There's no denying this man will be my end. Our connection is palpable, and I realize with certainty, I love him beyond reason. "You will feel me fill you. Mark you. Do you hear me, Petal? Come with me. Squeeze my dick with your gorgeous little cunt." He groans, and those words are my undoing. Trembling in his arms, hot jets of his seed shoot into me. He's now claimed and marked me, inside and out.

My body is the lyrics, and his the melody. Together our souls are a symphony. Between the love he gives me, and the fire that burns between us, we find euphoria as one.

CALLUM

I kept Tay from knowing where we're headed most of the flight. As we near our destination, the pilot makes the usual announcements. Then he mentions we're about to land in the Czech Republic. Her stare lands on me, and when I glance over at her, the excitement beaming off her is a light in a dark tunnel. "Prague!" Her voice is loud, and everyone turns to look at her. The blush on her cheeks is adorable.

"Yes, baby. Are you excited?" I ask the obvious.

"Oh my god, yes." She leans over and hugs me. Her sweet scent is incredibly sexy, and I'm hungry to get her alone and ravage every inch of her.

"Good. Because that's not the only surprise." We disembark and make our way through to customs. Being in another country calms me. There aren't any crazed fans or reporters. I do, however, receive VIP treatment at baggage claim. The car I scheduled is waiting as we exit the main terminal. Once the driver has loaded our luggage in the trunk, he drives through the beautiful city to our destination. I inhale a deep breath. There is something I have to collect as soon as we're settled. I need to figure out how to evade the questions I know she'll bombard me with.

I planned everything — a daily itinerary. Since we're only on vacation for a week, I needed to be sure we missed none of the sites. When we finally reach The Emblem Hotel, Tayla's eyes are wide with fascination. She looks like a kid on Christmas morning.

We're booked in the Suite Terrace, which is the biggest of the rooms. It has a private patio that overlooks the historic rooftops. The room is airy, modern, and beautiful. "Callum, this is gorgeous." Watching her wonderment makes me smile. To give her this, or anything else she wants, is my life's goal.

"Did you want to go sightseeing? Or relax? We're having dinner this evening with an acquaintance of mine." Her gaze snaps up.

"You have friends here?" I nod. It's not a complete lie. "Okay, I want to have a nap. The flight was exhausting."

"Sounds like a plan, Petal. There's something I need to collect. Stay here, and I'll be back as soon as I can." Her frown is adorable. "Don't worry." Planting a soft kiss on her forehead, I leave her. My heart is racing. At least I know the store will still be open. Thankfully.

As soon as I walk in, I find the jeweler who assisted me with my inquiry. "Mr. Hayes, welcome. Thank you for the order. It's been a pleasure to create this for you." He's a middle-aged man who I met when we toured here, and he's been an incredible help with the design I enquired about. He happily agreed to create the ring along with another small gift for Tay. This had to be perfect and rare. Unique.

"I'm delighted that you've been able to do it for me in the short time frame I gave." I pick up the two boxes and snap them both open. I can't believe it. It's precisely what I wanted. She will love it. I hope she doesn't consider it too expensive. The cost is irrelevant. This woman is my lover, my life.

"Do you like? We can change the crystals if you wish for a smaller set?" I shake my head.

"This is superb. I requested something original, and you delivered. Let me settle your payment. I need to get back to her." He nods, and I hand over my black credit card. He places both boxes in a gift bag for me. On my way to the hotel, my heart is pounding. Nerves are getting the better of me. Performing for millions of people is less stressful.

In the elevator up to the suite, my phone rings. When I glimpse at the name on screen, I hit the green button. "Good afternoon, sir."

"Callum. We've arrived. Thank you for the tickets and setting us up. It's wonderful."

"My pleasure. Dinner is at eight, so we will see you later."

"Excellent. Did you have a decent flight?"

"Yes, sir. We're both going to relax. I made a quick stop at the jewelers."

"I anticipate you will show it to us?" His voice is steady, but I realize he's anxious.

"Yes, tonight."

"Good. See you later." We say our goodbyes, and I stride down the hallway to the room.

As soon as I step through the door, I discover my lovely woman sitting on the balcony. She's dressed in a big, floppy, woolen jersey. Her one shoulder is exposed, showing off her intricate tattoo. Her sleek, ice-blonde hair hangs loose. She is curled up on the bench facing the city. Before she turns, I hide the pouch from the store in the safe.

When I approach the terrace, she peers at me, regarding me with suspicion. "Are you hiding something from me, Hayes?" I recognize her annoyed tone, but it's for a good reason.

"Yes, I am. But you need to trust me. I assure you, you'll be happy when you find out what it is." She draws a deep gulp of the white wine, and her lips glisten. I ache to taste it from her mouth. Or her body. She looks so serene and relaxed.

"If you say so." She darts her eyes forward to the view ahead and stares off into nothing.

"Are you okay, darling?"

"Just sleepy. Thank you for bringing me here, Callum. I have always wanted to see Prague. It's so romantic here. The old-world buildings are surreal."

"It is. And I expect that this vacation will be eternally etched in your mind." Peering at my phone, I realize we don't have a lot of time before we have to be at the restaurant. "I'm going to shower and get ready for dinner." Spinning on my heel, I make my way into the bathroom. Stripping off, I turn on the taps and watch the mirror steam up. As I step in the hot spray, it hits my shoulders, cascading down my body. Lowering my head under the water, I close my eyes and picture Tay smiling at me. I want this week to be perfect, and it will be — only if Tayla doesn't run.

I sense her behind me before she touches me. Her arms steal around my torso, and her breasts are warm against my back. A growl escapes my lips, and she accepts that as an invitation. Her hands lower to my abs, then she reaches for my cock. Gripping it firmly, she fists it in a gradual up and down motion. I'm solid steel. A need to plunge inside her takes hold of me.

Her movements are torturous. She is driving me insane. I'm about to explode with tension when I let out a hiss. "Jesus, woman, you're killing me." With my hand engulfing hers, I stroke faster.

"Callum. Please fuck me?" She releases me,

and when I twist round to her, the tears on her face rip my heart from my chest.

"Baby, what's wrong?" My hands cup her face, tilting it up, so her eyes meet mine.

"Nothing. I need you. Please?" I reach down and grab her ass, lifting her as she wraps her legs around my waist. There's no point in making sure she's ready because when the crown of my cock touches her slick entrance, it slides in effortlessly. Her hips roll forward as she rides me. I pin her against the wall, thrusting into her.

She hold onto me. Her eyes are shut so tight I'm sure she can see stars. The only thing I can do is fuck her exactly as she asked me to. "Harder, Callum. Faster. Deeper. Make me come." Her moans and words spur me on. I'm so confused and turned on, but my hips move faster as I plow into her. "Yes." Her cries are loud. "Callum, yes. Fuck." Her pussy tightens and pulses, and her sweet nectar floods my shaft, and I can't stop my release filling her deep.

I hold her there for what feels like hours. "Baby?" Her soft chestnut eyes are filled with sadness. She offers me a small smile.

"I love you, Callum." My heart thuds at her words.

"I love you too, but you're scaring me."

"Today is the fifth anniversary of what happened. That night." The emotion heavy in my throat threatens to choke me.

"Jesus, why didn't you tell me sooner?"

"I couldn't." I let her down slowly, and

my mouth molds with hers. Soft, sweet, and everything I feel for her pours from me as my tongue claims her mouth. Her hands twist in my hair, pulling me closer. Our bodies are so close we could be one person. Everything I need or want is right here. The love that fills my heart flows through me, and I try showing her with my body, lips, hands, and tongue.

After our shower, we get ready for dinner and head to the restaurant. The maître d' escorts us to the table I booked. I seat Tayla with her back to the door, so she can't see who walks in. The waiter brings the wine and the champagne I requested. "Are we celebrating?" she questions. I nod.

"Yes, we are. I planned the whole week as a surprise, but also as a way of showing you how much I love you. I know money isn't everything, but I have it, and I want to spoil you. So, I bought you a gift." I pull out the bigger gift and hand it to her.

"Callum Hayes, I told you not to waste money on me."

"It's only wasting if you don't want it. Open it." I gesture to the velvet box. She snaps the top, and a gasp leaves her lips, sending an electric jolt to my cock.

"Cal. This is . . ." She pulls out the necklace and pendant. Customized for her, angel wings, the only variation is that the one wing comprises vines and cherry blossoms with tiny pink diamonds in them. It matches her tattoo exactly. The other wing is intricately engraved in white gold.

"Do you like it, Petal?" She nods, and when her eyes meet mine, they're brimming with tears. I reach over and help her put it on. It's so dainty on her neck. The colors of the gems sparkle in the low light, and on her skin, the white gold looks exquisite.

Just then, my gaze falls on the door, and our guests arrive. "Our dinner party have arrived." I stand as Mr. and Mrs. Quinn walk up to our table. If I had a camera to capture Tayla's expression, I would have framed the beautiful photo. Her face lights up like the Empire State building on New Years'.

"Dad! Mom!" She jumps up and gives them both a long hug. She snaps her stare up. "You did this?"

I nod. "I figured you needed family time." We all take our seats, and I slip into the chair next to Tayla. She's seated between her mother and me. They both offer me a warm smile.

"How?" She darts her gaze between them and me.

"I got your parents' number from Emma, and since they were in London, I invited them out to see you before we head back to LA."

We're almost through dinner, and everything is going smoothly. Her father seems to be content with my answers about looking after Tayla, and her mom is wonderful. Just like my girl. I notice where Tay gets her beauty from. When they leave for the restrooms, I hand the other box I have for Tayla to Mr. Quinn.

He opens it and peers at it for a long while. My heart constricts in my throat; hoping he approves. With a snap, he closes it and hands it back. Our eyes meet, but he hasn't responded. Just then, the ladies join us. I'm on edge as his approval would mean a lot. His daughter is the love of my life.

"Callum, darling, if you don't mind. I think Richard and I will leave now. Thank you for everything, but I'm getting tired, and I don't want to stay out too late. You and my baby have a delightful evening." She presents an affectionate smile, and the pointed look she gives her husband is evidence enough she recognizes how this night will play out.

"Yes, we're heading to the hotel. Callum, it's been a pleasure meeting you. You take care of my angel." He reaches out a hand, and I grasp it. With a firm shake, the nod he gives is unmistakable. "I admire you, son. We will visit you soon." When he draws me in for a brief hug, his tone is low. "You have my blessing." My chest almost bursts with happiness.

"Thank you so much. That means

everything." Once they've left, Tayla sits quietly sipping her wine. I can't help watching her. Every movement she makes is refined. Beautiful. Delicate.

"Petal, are you okay?"

"Cal, that was incredible. Nobody has done anything like that for me. I love you." Her words are sincere. She's missed them. It must be rough being so far from your parents — especially today of all days. The MC steps up and persuades people to dance. The first song I would recognize anywhere. Kerli was an artist I worked with on two songs. Her release "Chemical" was just starting, and I needed my girl with me.

"Dance with me, Ms. Quinn." I rise and offer her my hand. When she slips hers in mine, I draw her up, and we make our way to the nearly empty dance floor. The lyrics are perfect for how I feel about my extraordinary woman. My love for her is more than physical; it's embedded in my soul.

> *Open up my eyes and feel your heartbeat*
> *As we lay with your body pressed against mine*
> *And I know, and I know this very moment*
> *This will be, this will be till the end of time*
> *I want you to know*
>
> *This love is more than chemical*
> *It feels unusual*
> *And I can't get enough*
> *You know-oh-oh*
> *This love is more than chemical*

And we're unbreakable
Oh be forevermore
More than chemical

Every time the darkness falls around me
I can feel you move beneath my skin
Eh and
Something strange is happening inside me
Don't know where you end and I begin
I want you to know

As the song comes to an end, I realize it's time. This is it. When I first saw Tayla walk into my house, I knew I had to have her. You see, there's something I've never told anyone before. Love for me was something I believed I should stay away from. When I saw the pain my mother went through after my father left, I promised myself love was something I would rather not have. Now that I have Tay in my life, I want love. I want everything I was so afraid to feel.

As she steps back, I stop her by holding her wrist. "Wait." Her face is passive as I drop to one knee in the middle of the busy restaurant. Everyone is still chatting and eating, but as soon as the whispers travel around the room, everyone stops. They're all watching us.

"Callum, what are you doing?" Her blush is beautiful. I want her to blush for me every day for the rest of my fucking life. The MC holds the mic out to me, and I grab it with one hand, holding Tay's with the other.

"Tayla Quinn, you stumbled into my life.

Literally. It's been almost five months of an intense and wild ride. We've been through a lot, and somehow, you're still here with me. I don't know why." The crowd laughs, but they hang on to every word. So does she. "I never wanted love. The fear of seeing what my mother went through made me a cynical bastard. I went through life thinking women were just there for entertainment. I didn't involve feelings or my heart."

Her breathing hitches and tears fill her eyes. "That is until you strolled into my life, and threw a mug of coffee over me. You ordered me not to be intrusive and interrupt you while you're speaking. Until you forced me to realize that love isn't something I should be scared of, but something I need to embrace with both hands. Now, as I kneel before you, I need to accept not only you, but us, with both hands. You're the lyrics to my song, the melody to my life, and the symphony to my forever. Tayla Quinn, will you do me the honor of being Mrs. Callum Hayes and be my wife? Be my happy ending?"

The place is so quiet you could hear a pin drop. Everyone is holding their breath. So am I. She's silent while her gaze wanders over me, then to our enthusiastic audience. We're all waiting with bated breath. I want to say something more, but I prefer not to interrupt her. When her gaze settles on me then, she grins and nods.

"Yes, Callum." Two of the most magnificent words I ever heard. The crowd applauds, and the MC grabs the mic from me. I pull my girl into me, picking her up and twirling her around.

"Cal?"

"Yes, baby?"

"Do I get a ring?" My loud chuckle echoes through the restaurant. Letting her down. I tug the box from my pocket. Snapping it open, I grasp out the elegant white gold ring. It's also custom designed. A solitaire white diamond surrounded by pink diamonds. As quickly as it slips onto her finger, the music starts, and the announcement of our engagement is made.

I don't know how long we danced that night, but I can tell you, by the time I took my fiancée to the bedroom, I wasn't tired when I stripped her out of the beautiful dress she wore and made love to her till the sun came up.

EPILOGUE

<u>Callum</u>

The music room is quiet tonight, and I enjoy the welcome silence. We've just finished filming our latest video, and I need to take a few days off. It's been three weeks since Tay, and I got engaged, and she has been busy trying to finalize the wedding plans. Kierra has been incredible with the schedule, venues, and everything else my woman needs.

As I take a seat on the bench in front of the piano, I inhale a long, deep breath. There's a song I've been working on for the ceremony. I want to surprise her, and I only have time to write when my angel isn't here. She's sneaky though. She found my notebook the other night, wanting to know what I was writing.

We've decided on warm weather for our celebration, so we have set a date in summer. We have rented a winery in Napa. It's romantic, beautiful, and we will stay after the reception. The girls have been shopping for dresses nonstop, and Tayla has her mind on something particular. I can't wait to feast my eyes on her in the dress. And out of it too.

"Cal." Her soft, sweet voice tugs me from dirty thoughts and vivid images.

"What's up, Petal?" Twisting to face her, I notice she's dressed in a floor-length, charcoal dressing gown. It's new; I haven't seen it before. "You buy that today?" She nods, shutting the door. She turns the lock with a soft click.

"I wanted to say hi. I missed you." Her tentative steps toward me allow me to take her in fully. The robe is sheer, and in the dim light of the lamps behind her, her curves are visible through the satin material. An exquisite sight and my cock agrees, throbbing in agony against my zipper.

"I missed you too, gorgeous." She reaches up and slips off the thin robe. The lump in my throat nearly suffocates me as I try to swallow past it. She's wearing a tiny black thong, matching corset, and a garter belt. I didn't notice it earlier, but she also has a pair of black heels on her feet. "Fuck."

"You like?"

"Jesus, Tayla, I fucking love." My groan is evidence enough that my lust for her is through the roof. Her sweet giggle sends electric currents to my dick. I'm aching to fill her tight, wet cunt. "Come over here." She complies. As soon as she's standing between my thighs, my hands hold onto the backs of her knees. "Lean over."

When she does, I have an incredible view of her luscious tits.

Chestnut eyes stare at me, waiting for my next command. "Do you enjoy making me hard for you?" Her nod is brief, and her pupils dilate as I caress her legs. I grip her hips, pushing her back. Rising from my seat, we're now face to face. Or face to chest. She's a head shorter than me, and when I glance down, the beautiful cleavage has a low groan rumbling in my throat.

"Cal . . ."

"Shh, Petal. I'm in charge. I want you to hold onto the edge of the piano. You will bend over, till your sexy little ass is poised for me. Then you are to spread your legs wide. Do you understand me?"

"Yes, Callum." A smirk tugs at the corner of my mouth. I step backward and watch her lean forward. It's taken all my strength not to spank her creamy skin or rip that tiny scrap of material from her body and ram inside her. The room is so quiet, and her breaths are the only thing I hear; and they're becoming harsher. The anticipation of what I'm about to do is turning her on.

Unzipping my jeans, I drop them to the floor and tug my tee off. I'm standing in a pair of briefs and nothing else. I pad toward her. With a tight grip on her hips, I press my rigid cock against her ass. "Cal . . . Please?" Without warning, I raise my hand, bringing it down on her peach ass. The red print appears, and I can't help smiling. *Mine.*

"What, Petal? You came in here for something tonight. You want my cock, darling? You need me to fill your tight little pussy deep and hard?"

"Yes. I do."

I rain a second swat on the other cheek of her porcelain flesh. Her long hair is loose. Perfect. Fisting it, I pull her up against me. "You ache for me? Like this?" Thrusting my erection between her ass cheeks again earns me a sexy whimper. When she pushes against me, I know she's probably dripping. "My naughty little angel is wet for me, isn't she?"

Her head moves in what I can only assume to be a nod. "Be quiet, okay?" Another attempt at agreeing with me, and I push her over on the black, shiny wood of the piano. With a swift move, I rip the thong from her body. Her gasp is louder than I want, which earns her two more swats.

But when I squat behind her, it's me who groans loudly. Her sweet nectar scent intoxicates me. With my tongue flat against her, I lick her long and slow. *Fuck!* My dick is throbbing painfully. I can't handle it anymore. Rising, I shove my briefs off, and without a word, plunge deep into her. To the hilt. The sexy noises that escape her mouth have me pulsing inside her.

Pulling out and slamming back in, my body trembles. Again, and again. I'm coiled so tight I may snap. "Cal . . . Cal . . . um . . ." Her broken words rip me from a haze of lust. "I ache for you everywhere." It takes a minute for her request to sink into my sex-fueled brain. My thumb circles the puckered hole I've been dying to claim.

"Here, baby? You want me to take your tight little ass?" There are no words, only a nod. I pull out of her sopping pussy, sliding two fingers into her. Using her arousal as a lubricant, I tease the incredibly tight hole. She's so fucking tight I won't last long.

My fingers slip into her slowly. "Relax, baby. I need you calm. Okay?" She nods again. My fingers slide into her ass. As soon as she relaxes, my fingers slide in easily. She trusts me with her body. It's the biggest turn on ever.

When I nudge her with the crown of my shaft, she whimpers. Slowly, I work the tip into her. "That's it, baby. Just relax." My fingers slide into her pussy and flick her clit, tweaking it, taking her concentration off my cock and onto what my hand is doing. She relaxes as I inch my way deeper. Slow. Methodical. As soon as I slip into the tightest part of her, my eyes roll back. *Jesus, fuck!* "God, Tay, you feel so good. So fucking good."

"Fuck me, Callum. Please?" That's what I needed to hear. My body moves of its own volition. Sliding in and out. Faster. Harder. Slower. My mind is blank. All that matters is our joined bodies. My grip on her hips will leave a bruise; there's no doubt. My cock pistons into her. "Yes, Cal. I'm close." Those four words bring me to the edge. I reach around and tweak her hard bud with my thumb and forefinger, sending her crashing into the abyss with me. My Angel. My Petal. Forever.

OTHER BOOKS

Stand Alones
Choosing the Hart
Love Beyond Words
Cuffed
Fragile Innocence
Perfectly Flawed
Black Light: Obsessed
Among Ash and Ember
Within Me (Limited Time)
Cursed in Love (collaboration with Cora Kenborn)
Beautifully Brutal (Cavalieri Della Morte)

Taboo Novellas
Sunshine and the Stalker (collaboration with K Webster)
His Temptation
Austin's Christmas Shortcake
Crime and Punishment (Newsletter Exclusive)
Malignus (Inferno World Novella)
Virulent (collaboration with Yolanda Olson)
Tempting Grayson

ABOUT DANI

Dani is a *USA Today* bestselling author of a variety of genres, from romantic suspense to dark erotic romance and even BDSM romance. She loves to delve into the raw, emotional journeys her characters venture on, and enjoys the dark, edgy, and sensual scenes that fill the pages of her books. Dani's stories are seductive with a deviant edge with feisty heroines and dominant alphas.

Dani lives in the beautiful city of Cape Town, and is a proud member of the Romance Writer's Organization of South Africa (ROSA) and the Romance Writers of America (RWA). She has a healthy addiction to reading, TV series, music, tattoos, chocolate, and ice cream.

www.danirene.com
info@danirene.com